"Though your sins are like scarlet,
they shall be as white as snow;
though they are red as crimson,
they shall be like wool."

—Isaiah 1:18 (NIV)

Extraordinary Women OF THE BIBLE

HIGHLY FAVORED: MARY'S STORY
SINS AS SCARLET: RAHAB'S STORY

Extraordinary Women OF THE BIBLE

SINS AS SCARLET

RAHAB'S STORY

Beth Adams

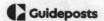

Extraordinary Women of the Bible is a trademark of Guideposts.

Published by Guideposts
100 Reserve Road, Suite E200
Danbury, CT 06810
Guideposts.org

Cover and interior design by Müllerhaus.

Cover illustration by Brian Call represented by Illustration Online LLC.

Typeset by Aptara, Inc.

ISBN 978-1-961441-60-6 (hardcover)
ISBN 978-1-961441-61-3 (softcover)
ISBN 978-1-959633-30-3 (epub)

Printed and bound in the United States of America

Extraordinary Women OF THE BIBLE

SINS AS SCARLET

RAHAB'S STORY

Cast of
CHARACTERS

RAHAB'S FAMILY

Anshar • Rahab's father
Omarosa • Rahab's mother

Kishar • Rahab's sister
  Abu-Waqar • Kishar's husband
  Hili • Kishar's daughter
  Gal • Hili's fiancé
  Ushi • Kishar's baby son
  Awil-Ili • Kishar's son
  Sagar • Kishar's son
  Abbi • Kishar's servant

Nuesh • Rahab's brother
  Olib • Nuesh's wife

Sagma •Rahab's brother

Gibil • Rahab's brother
  Erish • Gibil's wife
  Hedu and Gedri • Gibil's daughters

Ri • Rahab's sister

  Hirin • Ri's husband

  Zelah • Ri's daughter

OTHER CHARACTERS

Adrahasis • from Jerusalem, Rahab doesn't know his business

Alam • spice trader from the east

Garza • guest at the inn

Gishimar • guest at the inn, from Jerusalem

Haran • dried goat meat merchant

Hashur • metal trader

Hazi • guest who stays with Rahab regularly

Inanna • Kishar's friend who has a sister who makes robes for the palace

King Uz • King of Canaan

Kingu • Mashda's son

Mashda • Rahab's late husband

Minesh • Rahab's childhood sweetheart

Mostafa • vegetable seller who will sell to Rahab

Munzur •beggar at the city gate

Mylitta • widow at the well

Nirgal • metal trader

Penzer • tax collector

Salmon and Ronen • Israelite spies

Shenbar • Fruit seller who will not sell to Rahab

Tauthe • Kingu's wife

Tiamat • woman who sells milk and cheese

Ultultar • King Uz's brother, rightful heir

Yarikh • Canaanite moon god

CHAPTER ONE

Hazi was afraid. Even in the dim lamplight, Rahab could see it in his eyes as he stepped inside. The heavy wooden door slammed behind him, but he didn't seem to notice. The traders gathered around the table looked up from their stew and turned toward the sound.

"Welcome back." Rahab walked around the wooden table and toward the door to greet her guest. Hazi, a trader of furs and leather goods, traveled throughout the land and was one of her more frequent guests. He stayed at her inn whenever his business brought him to Jericho, and she often enjoyed hearing the stories of his travels and the people he met. But she could see that something was different tonight. It was in the set of his shoulders, the way he pressed his mouth into a thin line. "Let me take your cloak."

Hazi handed his traveling cloak to her without a word. This was very unlike him. Hazi was friendly and loved to talk, sometimes beyond Rahab's desire to listen, and he was never rude. Rahab hung his cloak on the hook by the door and guided him toward the long table.

"Your things are in the courtyard?" she asked.

He nodded. Hazi knew to tie up his donkey in the courtyard below the main floor of the inn before coming up the steps to the door. He would have left his cart there too. Rahab would lock the door as soon as the city gate was closed for the night.

"Please sit." She gestured toward the dining table, where her three other guests also sat. "Meet Alam, Hashur, and Adrahasis."

Hazi nodded to them but did not speak to them. Something was definitely wrong. This was so unlike him.

"You are in luck," she said, keeping her voice light. She walked back to the serving table, poured cool water into a thick earthenware cup, and carried it to him. The night was warm, and the cooking fire made it warmer. "There is lamb stew tonight."

Lamb stew was Hazi's favorite dish. He always asked for it when he stayed at her inn, though he knew she did not make it often. She only had meat when Haran gave her a good deal, but if Hazi knew that, he did not let on.

Hazi did not respond. He was looking down at his hands, jiggling his leg up and down beneath the table. The air inside the room had gone still, thick, choked with smoke and sweat and something else she couldn't identify. The pure animal scent of fear, maybe. She went back to the serving area and scooped a portion of the stew into a bowl and carried it to him.

"What is wrong?" She slid the stew in front of him. He looked up and nodded, thanking her. "What has you so frightened?"

Hazi didn't answer for a moment, but then he gestured to the bench across from him, indicating that she should sit down. Alam, the spice trader, scooted over so she could sit. It was not a large table, and the traders were all watching Hazi with interest.

"I have just come from the Valley of Moab." Hazi's eyes were wide. Rahab nodded. She knew that his trading route

2

often took him through all the cities in the region. There were several large cities in that area—Dibon, Heshbon, Jahaz—all of them with markets where Hazi had good luck trading. Hazi was a very wealthy man, to hear him tell it. "They are gone, all of them."

"Who is gone?" Rahab did not understand. Heshbon was a large, powerful city on the far side of the sea, several days' journey from here. It stood in the shadow of a mountain, and on the edge of a desert, and was said to be one of the richest and most powerful kingdoms in the land. Rahab had not been there. She had not been anywhere, but she heard about so many places from the travelers who came through the inn. Jericho was in the valley, on one of the main trading roads, and she hosted people from all over the world.

"The Amorites," Hazi stammered. "The people of Heshbon and all of the surrounding towns. The cities have been conquered. The people destroyed completely. All of them are dead."

"That's impossible," Alam said immediately.

Alam was right. King Sihon was one of the most powerful kings in the land, and Heshbon was an important city. It could not have been taken. It could never happen. And if it had, they would have heard.

"And yet it is true. I have seen it with my own eyes."

"What do you mean they have been conquered?" The metal trader, Hashur, turned to Hazi. He was thick and squat, with wide-set eyes and an easy laugh. Rahab had just met him that night, as he had not done business in Jericho before, but he'd declared the shared rooms perfectly suitable. He shook his head. "I am afraid you are mistaken. That is not possible. I was just there not two moons past."

"No one could conquer Heshbon," Alam added. Alam came from the east, carrying spices whose colors and aromas dazzled the eye and the nose. They held flavors Rahab could only imagine. "The Amorite king cannot be beaten. King Sihon is far too powerful. His cities have strong, thick walls, and his army numbers in the thousands. The city cannot be taken."

"Heshbon has been taken before," the third trader, Adrahasis, said. Adrahasis came from Jerusalem and had fine features and dark eyes that missed nothing. Rahab was not sure what his business was, only that he always paid up front for his stays and that he did not like to talk about what he did while he was in Jericho. "King Sihon himself took the city from the Moabite king."

"But King Sihon has armed his cities well," Hashur said. "The walls are guarded heavily. They say his army is invincible."

"They are wrong," Hazi said. Tiny wisps of steam rose up off the surface of the stew, but he didn't even seem to notice the food in front of him. "Heshbon is destroyed. I have seen it with my own eyes. King Sihon is dead, his army gone, the people all vanquished. The invading army settled in the area and then marched on. They have also taken Jazer and driven out all the people who are there—all the settlements as well."

"What would they want with Jazer?" Alam asked. "It is not a big city. Hardly worth taking."

"It is on the river," Adrahasis said, shrugging. "Good access to water." The oil lamp on the table cast flickering shadows over his face, making his expression appear dark.

Alam nodded, considering this.

But Hazi was not done yet. He spoke again. "After that they marched toward Bashan."

"Bashan?" Hashur questioned. "They went to Bashan?"

Rahab felt a stab of fear. The region of Bashan was much closer to Jericho, just two days' journey to the east. King Og, who ruled the area, was said to be a good king, kind to his people, not demanding too much in taxes nor treating his people badly. King Og had two royal cities, as well as sixty strongly fortified towns, under his control.

"Surely King Og defeated them," Alam said, though his voice betrayed the fear his words did not. "His army is strong, his cities secure."

"They say King Og met the invaders with his full army at Edrei." Hazi took a long drink from his cup, and when he set it down, his hands were shaking. Edrei was one of King Og's royal cities, and perched on a hill, surrounded by thick walls. "King Og was defeated, he and his sons and his whole army."

"No." Hashur could not seem to muster any more than this. Rahab understood why. It was unthinkable. Unbelievable. This invading army could not have struck down two of the most powerful kings in the land.

Rahab did not want to believe it. She could see the men at her table were struggling to believe it as well. She had never known Hazi to stretch the truth. But this seemed impossible. What people could have truly destroyed the kingdoms of the Amorites?

"But who are they?" Alam had already finished a second bowl of stew and was eyeing the pot as if hoping for more. "There is no army capable of such a thing."

"They are called the Israelites," Hazi said. "They also call themselves the Hebrews."

"The Israelites?" Alam said, shaking his head. "I have never heard of them. Surely we would have heard of them if they were powerful enough to do what you say."

"Their leader calls himself Joshua," Hazi said. "They claim their god has given them this land as their own."

Hashur laughed aloud at that. "Is their god more powerful than the other gods?"

"It is not possible," Alam said again, shaking his head.

"The Israelites?" Adrahasis had narrowed his eyes. "I have heard of the Israelites."

"*I* have never heard of them." Hashur crossed his thick arms over his chest. He narrowed his eyes and lifted his chin up.

Adrahasis continued. "I heard of them when I was at Kadesh. They are migrants. A pathetic, ragged bunch of wanderers. They have no homeland. They have been walking around for many years, with no direction, no plans. They set up camp in places no one else wants to stay. They certainly have no army capable of destroying the kingdoms of powerful kings like Sihon and Og."

"And yet, apparently, they do," Hazi said. "For they have taken the land for themselves and destroyed all who live within."

"It cannot be true," Alam said, shaking his head. He did not want to believe it. Rahab did not want to believe it either, but Rahab's life had taught her that denying unpleasant facts did not make them any less true.

"It is said their leader is considering where to go next," Hazi said. "He is sending out men to scout the whole land of Canaan, looking for his next conquest."

"He must be insane. Demented." Hashur's eyes were wide.

"It is greed," Alam added. "Pure greed."

"It would be a very stupid thing to do, to drive that ragtag army into a place like this," Adrahasis said. "He would be risking everything they have already gained."

"Canaan is not like those other places," Alam said. "The cities here are big. The kings are powerful. The armies here are well trained."

Rahab felt unease grow within her. If what Hazi said was true... If these Israelites and their god were powerful enough to do what Hazi said they had done... If this Joshua was planning to advance into Canaan...

"Do you think he will come to Jericho?" Rahab couldn't stop herself from asking.

No one answered for a moment, and in the stillness, Rahab heard the low groan of the city gate closing off the town for the night. No one seemed to know what to say. These men were traders. They wandered from place to place, calling no city home. Rahab had lived in Jericho her whole life. This was where her family was. If the Israelites came to Jericho—

"You do not need to worry," Hazi said quickly. "Even if they do come this way, the walls of Jericho are strong and thick." He leaned back and tapped the back wall of the room with his

7

hand. The inn was built into the city wall itself, and the back wall was made of rough plaster, which covered solid stone.

"Other armies have tried to take Jericho in the past," Adrahasis said. "None of them have succeeded."

Rahab knew he was right. Twice in her life, foreign kings had marched on the city, hoping to claim its fertile soil and green hills for themselves, but they had not succeeded either time. Still, scores had been lost in the fighting, and many had starved to death in the siege, when the gates had been sealed up tight.

"He is right," Alam said, gesturing toward Hazi. "You will be safe from the Israelites. Jericho is secure. Nothing could get through these walls."

Rahab took some comfort from his words, but she felt unsettled. She hoped he was right.

CHAPTER TWO

Rahab rose before the sun the next morning. She had slept poorly, and she felt groggy and slow as she made her way down the steps from the sleeping rooms to the dining area. She heard snoring coming from the room Adrahasis and Alam shared, and the downstairs room was empty. The air was warm already, and the sun was not yet up. It was still spring, but that did not seem to matter.

Rahab first took her jugs and carried them down the steps and into the street and then made her way to the well at the end of town. If she came early enough, she could often manage to avoid the other women, who ignored her in person but gossiped about her when she was not around. This day, she was glad to encounter only Mylitta, another widow who now lived with her husband's family in a cramped, loud home on the far side of the gate. Mylitta did not meet Rahab's eye, but she did not openly scorn Rahab.

Rahab waited until Mylitta was done, and then she filled her own jugs and balanced them carefully as she returned home. She was sweating by the time she walked the short distance and entered her house. She set the jugs down next to the ones filled with wine and oil, lit a fire, and began the rest of her morning chores. She mixed a little flour and yeast for bread, and then she sliced cheese and fruit to feed the men who lodged with her. She took a small piece of the bread dough and set it in front of the altar in the corner, her daily offering to Yarikh, the moon god whose home was Jericho. She asked for his blessing and for the means to pay her debts without going back to...what she'd been forced to do before.

When she heard the men stirring, she rose and set out yesterday's bread and the fruit and cheese. She tried to talk with the men as they ate, but each seemed to be preoccupied with his thoughts this morning. She wondered if they had spent the night worrying, as she had, about the Israelites, but she did not dare ask. They all left the inn early, each to his own business, and once they were gone, Rahab set the leftover food aside, cleaned up the table, and tidied the rooms. Rahab could not provide luxurious linens or rich meals, but she took pride in the fact that the inn was always clean and well kept.

Then, when everything was as it should be, she took her bag of coins from behind the loose brick in the chimney and tied it to the belt around her waist. She grabbed her cloak, filled a small linen bag with the table scraps, and set out.

When Rahab first moved to this part of town, just after her wedding, she had been surprised by the constant noise and the incessant bustle here. Where she had grown up, on the far side of town, in the shadow of the palace, the streets were wider, and the houses were bigger and made of fine strong bricks and surrounded by palms and sycamores, which cast abundant shade over the houses. The servants had been sent out to run to the market, saving the family from having to go out in the heat of the day. The streets on this end of town were narrow, and pressed up close on both sides were homes that had been haphazardly built of stones and mud. Several of the houses along this stretch were abandoned and had fallen into disrepair, and the most unfashionable houses—including her own—were built right into the city wall. The road here was missing its stones in many places and was often slicked with mud and animal waste and worse. And there were so many people. All day and into the night, people from the homes that were packed closely together filled the narrow streets.

Today, as on most days, Rahab headed first to the city gates. The guards in their ramparts above had lowered the gate at daybreak so that now people came and went freely. Beyond the city walls, farmland stretched out, dotted with acacia trees and field grass, all the way to the river. But Rahab did not go out the gates. Instead, she walked up to Munzur, who was leaning up against the section in the wall just behind the gate, in the cool of the shade beneath the guards' watchtower.

"Good morning, Rahab." Munzur smiled when he saw her, his face twisting up into what she recognized as a crooked smile. Mashda had always said the man was not glad to see her, that he could not feel emotion, that he was only happy because she always brought him breakfast, but Rahab knew better. Munzur's legs and arms did not move right. He had used a walking stick from a young age, and his speech was slurred and could be difficult to understand, but he knew everything that went on around the city gates. Some said Munzur's difficulties came because he

11

had been possessed by demons. Others said his mother had mated with a demon to create him. Whatever the cause, Munzur could not work and was forced to beg at the city gates for food. Most mornings, Rahab brought him scraps of food left from her table, and he always seemed grateful.

"Good morning, Munzur. How are you today?" His name meant "bitter herbs," and from the beginning, his differences had been feared. Rahab reached into her bag and pulled out the crust of bread the guests had left on the table, as well as a few dried figs. His hands shook, as they always did, as he took them and immediately shoved the bread into his mouth.

"I am doing all right," he said through a mouthful of bread. "The guards? Well, that is a different story." He laughed a little.

"Why is that?" Rahab did not want to laugh at the guards' distress, though she understood how Munzur could. She knew they treated him worse than the dogs that roamed the streets. They would spit on him and toss garbage at him when they passed.

"They have been told to be on guard against visitors. It is believed spies will try to enter the city."

"Spies?" Because the guards believed Munzur was less than human, they did not bother to censor their talk as they passed him. Not only that, the guards were known to sometimes drink too much wine to pass the time, and their tongues loosened after that. And Munzur knew everything they spoke about, as well as every other person who came in and out of the city.

"Sent by the Hebrews." He took another big bite of the bread. "You have heard how they took the cities ruled by Sihon and Og?"

"I have," Rahab said. Goodness. Word about these Israelites was spreading fast, and if the guards had been told to be on watch, King Uz was worried. "They are said to be powerful."

"They are wicked, the guards say. Possessed by a demon they worship as a god, greedy to consume everything they see." Munzur shrugged and swallowed the bit of food in his mouth. "That is what the guards say, anyway."

"I hope they do not come here," Rahab said, feeling the same prickle of fear she'd felt last night.

Munzur laughed again. "It would be something to see, at least, would it not?"

Rahab did not think the destruction of their city was something she wanted to see. But she reminded herself that Munzur was a man with nothing to lose. He did not have family or friends he cared for. Rahab was not the same. She had neither husband nor children, nor did she have her good reputation or a high place in society, but she did have family she cared about. She had parents and brothers and a sister who loved her, no matter how far she'd fallen or what she'd done.

"Have a good day, Munzur," she said, turning back toward the city streets. He laughed as she walked away. So many avoided talking to Munzur, as if they worried they might catch whatever it was that made him different. Rahab knew she was not so very different. She had come dangerously close to being forced to beg at the city gates herself. She had only been spared that fate by the terrible truth that a woman always had one last thing to sell.

She headed back past her inn and threaded her way through the crowded passageways toward the section of the city where the king's officials worked. The palace, perched high on a hill and surrounded by palms, looked down on the city, its golden stone walls gleaming in the sun. The temple, where all were required to make their sacrifices to the gods, sat just beyond. Down here in the narrow streets, she passed a man leading a goat by a rope and a woman who was bent over, balancing a heavy load in a bag on her back. Somewhere in one of the houses, a woman was singing, the sound drifting out the window opening and echoing in the alleys. Linens hung from ropes strung across the small space between the buildings. She threaded through the small warren of streets until she came to the area where the king's tax collectors and building planners and other city employees worked, tucked away in tall buildings made of heavy blocks of smooth limestone. The tall wooden door of the tax collector's office was fortified with strips of iron and was designed to look tall and imposing. Rahab pushed open the door tentatively and stepped inside.

The small space was cool and quiet. A man sat hunched over a desk, writing numbers on a scroll in dark ink. The air held the sharp, pungent scent of poppy resin. Penzer had always loved to smoke the foul stuff, and the scent of opium clung to him. Mashda had loved it too. Penzer looked up and frowned.

"I trust you have the full amount this time?" His robes were woven of fine blue linen, and his beard was oiled and neatly trimmed, but the hair on his head had retreated and his skin was scarred from the pox that had swept through the town when he was a child.

"I don't have it all, Penzer."

14

He flinched when she used his name, but she did not hesitate. She knew him, knew who he truly was, and she would not be cowed by his position.

"However, I do have some." She reached for the bag tied to the cord at her waist and pulled out three coins. She set them on the table before him. He did not move to touch them. "I hope this will satisfy until I can bring the rest."

"This barely covers the penalty you must pay for being so late with the rest," Penzer said. There was nothing but disdain in his voice. Rahab steeled herself. If he felt disgust when he saw her, it was not her business. He was the one whose appetites had led him to offer her a way to cancel her debts. It was Penzer who had cheated the king, not she. He was the one who used his position to pressure a desperate woman to make a terrible choice. She would not have chosen that path had he not made it clear it was the only way out of Mashda's debt that would have taken the inn and everything else she owned. If seeing her face was a reminder that his own desires had caused him to betray his wife and king for fleeting pleasure, it was not her business.

"I will have more soon."

"You say that every time." The relief from the debt had been short-lived. The few fumbling encounters—she was filled with shame and disgust at the memories—had brought a short respite, but once Rahab had told Penzer she would no longer be paying her taxes by selling her body, Penzer had increased the taxes he charged her twofold. There was no way she could afford them, and he knew it. She did not know whether it was meant as punishment or as a way to entice her to change her mind, but in either case she would not waver.

"And I bring you more each week."

"I cannot keep letting you get away with this, Rahab. You must pay your taxes, or I will be forced to take action."

"I will find the money."

He knew she could never pay what she owed.

"Make sure you do. I cannot protect you forever." He did nothing to protect her, and they both knew it. He let his eyes wander up and down her body greedily.

"I will bring it shortly." She turned and walked out of the office before he could say anything more, letting the door slam shut behind her. Rahab took in deep gulps of air and walked away as quickly as she could. She did not know how she would pay off her debt, but she did know she would never let him near her body again.

Rahab made her way to the marketplace, located in a big open space at the center of the town. The marketplace was loud, crowded, and colorful, packed with stalls, one on top of the other, selling everything under the sun. Rahab walked past the metalworker, the leather tanner, and the carpenter, past the woman telling fortunes and the man selling finely woven rugs, toward the side where the food was sold. She walked past Shenbar's stand, piled high with beautiful fruits grown on his family's orchards just outside the gates. Delicate apricots and ruby-red pomegranates were set in baskets, along with overflowing baskets of figs and dates. Shenbar's fruit was the best—the sweetest, juiciest, and, he claimed, the most nutritious. But Rahab walked past, and Shenbar kept his eyes lowered. He would not look her way. Since word had gotten around about her dark times, Shenbar had refused to serve her or even speak to her. Rahab tried not to let his judgment bother her, but it still hurt. They had once been friends. Today, she walked on past his stall and headed for the stall at the end, where Mostafa sold fruit and other goods the other merchants could not sell, at a discount. His fruit was usually bruised, his vegetables limp, his grains starting to mold, but his prices were quite reasonable. And he was one of the few merchants who would do business with her. When one had few choices, she took what she could get.

Mostafa smiled as she walked up. "Good morning, Rahab. How are you this fine day?"

"Just fine, Mostafa." Mostafa had come to Jericho from Egypt many moons ago, long enough that he had made the city his home, but his darker skin and his accent marked him as different, which did not sit well with many in town. "And you?"

"I am alive and well, thanks be to the gods," Mostafa said. "What are you in the mood for today? I have some lovely peaches, and for you, a good price."

Rahab looked over the basket of peaches and found none that weren't bruised and starting to rot. The melons looked all right, though. She looked over the vegetables he had—bruised onions, dirty leeks, bitter greens wilting under the hot sun.

"I will have two melons," she said. "Also some wheat and a scoop of the lentils." She pointed to the pile of small brown discs on the table.

17

"Coming right up." Mostafa poured the lentils and ground wheat into the small containers she had brought, and she tucked the two heavy melons into her bag. She handed him her coins, and he tucked them into the small coin purse at his waist. "You have a very good day, Rahab."

"Thank you, Mustafa." The foreigner always treated her kindly, and she gave him a smile before heading toward Haran, the man who sold salted and cured meats. When she could not afford fresh meat, cured lamb or goats would often satisfy the travelers who stayed with her. She bought some dried goat meat, which she could cut up and cook with the lentils to make a meal that would fill their bellies, at least. The man at the stall kept his eyes averted and would not speak to her, but he took her money. She tucked the goat meat into her bag. With sliced melon and her fresh bread and strong drink, they might not realize how meager her offerings truly were.

She then turned and kept walking and went right past Tiamat, the woman who sold milk and cheeses. Tiamat used to be friendly and chatty, sharing stories about her grandchildren and her husband's overbearing mother, but she had stopped selling to Rahab after word got out about Penzer and the others. Rahab would get the milk and cheese from her mother and her sister, who both bought it in the market for her.

Her shopping done, Rahab made her way toward the far end of the market. Before heading home, she would stop in and pick up cheese from her sister Kishar, who lived not far from the home where Rahab had grown up. She pressed through the crowd, keeping her eyes downcast, until she heard the whisper.

"*Harlot.*"

Rahab whirled around, but she could not tell which of the dozens of bodies around her had said the word. It could have been any of them. They all knew what she had done. What she had, for a short time, been forced to do. She turned back, telling herself not to get upset, not to give them the satisfaction of seeing her anger, and she somehow managed to keep her face placid when she heard it again.

"*Harlot.*"

This time she did not turn. Instead, she hurried out of market, trying to keep her breath steady. It was the same, always. They would never forget that for a time, after her husband had died and left exorbitant debts, she had been forced to make a choice between violation and starvation. She had not welcomed it. She had not wanted it. What woman would choose to offer herself up to strangers? It had been awful, vile, the worst time in her life. And yet, faced with the alternative of starving, she had done what she had to do. She was certain any woman in the town would have done the same if she had been in her shoes. And, she could not help but think, if any one of them had been willing to help her, they could have prevented her from facing such a terrible choice. But none had been willing to offer her the loan she had needed to keep the debt collectors from taking everything. Those who judged her so harshly now had not shown her the kindness to help her avoid such a fate. She held her head up as she made her way out of the market. She would not let them see how much their words still hurt.

Rahab was not proud of her past. She knew her actions had made her unacceptable in polite society. She knew she had brought shame upon her family. And she wanted to scream at those who whispered about her in the market that she had not wanted it, that she had hated every moment of it. But because of it, she was alive. She was alive, and she had her inn, and she knew that if she were faced with the decision all over again, she would make the same choice. Any one of them would.

CHAPTER THREE

Rahab pushed her way through to the far side of the market, and the crowds thinned as she turned down the side streets near her old home. She did not turn toward the home of her family, though, and instead made her way to the familiar doorstep of Kishar. Rahab knocked on the door and was immediately welcomed inside by a servant and shown to the open courtyard at the center of the home. Olive and palm trees and myrtle brought life and color into the space.

"Good morning, Auntie." Hili was weaving on a small loom in the sunshine. She used fine thread dyed a deep crimson, and her weaving was neat and precise. No doubt working on an item she would bring with her to her new home when she was married this summer. Hili set down her thread and walked toward Rahab to give her a hug. "It is good to see you."

"You are looking well," Rahab said, pulling back to get a better look at her niece. She had a glow in her cheeks and a brightness in her eyes. "Very well, in fact." Rahab watched her niece's cheeks pinken, and she gave her a wink. "I see. You have been to see Gal then?"

Hili nodded, pressing her lips together. "We met last night, in the park behind the palace."

Memories flooded back to Rahab. She had been young and in love once too. She had risked her own father's wrath to meet the man she had hoped to marry. She would have risked anything to be with him. Nothing—not even a wise auntie who knew enough to worry—would have stopped her from meeting Minesh for their fleeting embraces.

"You must be careful your father does not find out." Abu-Waqar had always indulged Hili, his beautiful firstborn, and had arranged for a marriage to the man of Hili's choice. It was a love match, nearly unheard of, but he would not be pleased to find that Hili and Gal were meeting in secret before the wedding. If anything was to go wrong… "And you must not—"

Rahab broke off. Kishar's family had always stood by Rahab, had always welcomed her and helped her, even in the dark times. But that did not mean that she of all people would be welcome to advise on matters of this sort.

"Please be careful," Rahab finished, and Hili nodded and ushered Rahab into the courtyard. She turned back to her weaving.

"Mama is just tending to Ushi," Hili said. "She will be here shortly, I am sure."

"How is he?" Ushi was Kishar's youngest, still a baby. Everyone had been surprised and delighted when the boy was born more than ten years after Awil-Ili and twelve years after Sagar, Hili's younger brothers.

"Loud," Hili said, grimacing. "But he is very cute."

"He is that." Rahab nodded. She tried to stifle the pang of jealousy she often felt for her sister's many fine children. Rahab loved her sister and her children dearly, but that did not make it any easier that she had never been able to raise one of her own. "And your other brothers?"

"At the palace." Hili waved her hand dismissively. "Papa has them training like men. Mama thinks it is too soon, but—"

"But your father is wise and can be trusted." Rahab recognized the voice of her sister, Kishar. Rahab turned and saw Kishar coming toward them, Ushi on her hip.

"We must not question his decisions," Kishar continued, giving her daughter a knowing look.

"Hello, sister." Rahab walked toward Kishar and hugged her, and then she pulled Ushi into her arms. The child laughed and came to her willingly. Rahab buried her face in the baby's neck, inhaling his sweet scent.

"Hello, Rahab." Kishar took a seat on the bench in the shade under the olive tree and invited Rahab to do the same. "How are you?"

"I am all right," Rahab said. She blew kisses at her nephew, who grabbed a handful of her hair. She carefully worked his fingers free. "I have had many paying guests these past few weeks, so that helps."

"I am glad." Kishar stretched out her long legs beneath her skirts. "Has Kingu been bothering you again?"

Kingu was the son of Rahab's late husband, Mashda. Kingu had moved his family to Joppa, many days' journey from Jericho, when he took a second wife from that city. Rahab knew that was the only reason Kingu hadn't taken possession of the house she lived in after Mashda had passed three years ago. By rights, Kingu owned the house now, and he had threatened many times to take possession of it and to leave his father's second wife without a home. But so far, Kingu had not bothered to make the journey to take possession of the home, and Rahab prayed that he would continue to stay away.

"He sent a message a few weeks past," Rahab said. She bounced Ushi on her knee. "He suggested I sell the home and send him the money."

"He does not have need of the money," Kishar said. It was true—while Mashda had been but a struggling innkeeper, Kingu had built a thriving importing business and had more than enough.

"He does not have need of the home either," Rahab said. Ushi started to fuss, so she handed him back to Kishar, who set the child down on the ground.

"He was always a hateful person," Kishar said, shaking her head. "I wonder what happened to him to make him so awful. Mashda was not like that."

"I think his mother's death was difficult for him." Rahab tried her best to be charitable to her stepson, despite it all. "And he did not expect his father to marry again so quickly."

"He did not like that his father's few resources were being used on you instead of him," Kishar said. "And no doubt he was jealous that his father had a more beautiful wife than he did."

"Kishar."

"What? We both know it is true. Tauthe has a nose like a pig's. It is no wonder he took a second wife."

"Kishar, please."

"And you are the most beautiful woman in this city. Everyone knows it. Father acts like Mashda was so generous in marrying you after Father squandered your dowry, but we all know he was the one getting a good deal."

Rahab did not like to talk badly of anyone. Kishar could sit here in her walled garden in her fine house and dismiss the people of this town, but Rahab did not have that luxury. She was on shaky ground as it was, and if word got around to the wrong person, Rahab could be out on the street. She changed the subject.

"Hili said Awil-Ili and Sagma are training at the palace already?"

Kishar let out a sigh. "Gibil has called all available men to train. Apparently, King Uz is worried. There is some army said to be advancing into Canaan, and the king wants to build up Jericho's defenses."

"But they are not men, they are boys. Surely Gibil did not mean to call his nephews to battle." Rahab tried to keep her voice down so Hili would not hear. It was one thing for her sister's husband Abu-Waqar to fight to protect their city. He was a member of the king's guard, and a respected soldier. But Awil-Ili and Sagar were too young. Gibil, Rahab and Kishar's oldest brother, was head of the king's guard. Surely he could make exemptions for his nephews.

"That is what I told Abu-Waqar too. But it is not up to me. He says they are needed." A soft breeze picked up a strand of Kishar's hair, and she smoothed it back. The sweet scent of jasmine filled the air. "I do not know. I do not see what they are so worried about. The city walls are impregnable. They will protect us from any army."

Rahab would have assumed the same thing herself if she had not heard the stories Hazi told last night. But she would not burden Kishar with what she had heard. It would only worry her sister. And Gibil, despite everything, was a formidable fighter. He would train the king's army well.

"How is Gibby?" Rahab asked.

"Gibil is the same." Kishar waved her hand dismissively. "Imperious. Obnoxious. Thinks he's better than everyone else. As he always has."

"And Ri?"

"Ri spends too much time worrying about what others think of her. But aside from that, she is fine. She sends her love."

It was kind of Kishar to say so, but Rahab knew it was not true. Her sister Ri had not spoken to Rahab since news of what Rahab had stooped to in her desperation became public. Ri did not want to be associated with a fallen woman, even if she had been Ri's once-treasured baby sister. Ri acted as though her own good name would be spoiled by any connection with Rahab. Gibil was the same. They had both cut her out of their lives, when it all came out. Neither had offered to help her, to help alleviate the crushing poverty that had driven her to sleep with men for money, but they were quick to judge her for it. Rahab supposed she should be glad Kishar, as well as their other two brothers, risked their good names and still spoke to Rahab.

"How are Nuesh and Sagma? Do you hear from them?" Rahab and Kishar's brothers had been born together, and they had always spent most of their time together, and now they ran the ironworks together, making plates of armor for the king's army.

"Occasionally. They are so busy with their work and their families that I do not see them much." Kishar let out a sigh. "Is there anything you need?"

Rahab knew Kishar was asking out of kindness. But she hated the pity the question implied. Rahab would not tell her about the tax bill she owed. Her sister could not give her the money Abu-Waqar kept securely locked away, and she would only worry.

"I do all right. Let us hope the fine spring weather continues to bring travelers." Rahab then asked about plans for Hili's upcoming wedding, and while Ushi explored the yard on his hands and knees, Kishar told Rahab about the feast that was planned. Soon they had spent nearly an hour catching up. Rahab knew she must get back to the inn. There were always chores to be done. She stood to go, and Kishar gestured for her to follow her.

"Abbi was able to bargain for a good price this time," Kishar said, handing Rahab a block of cheese wrapped in a cloth that she'd retrieved from the cool of the cellar. "So there is more than usual."

"Thank you." Rahab tucked the block of cheese in her bag and took the jug of goat's milk Kishar held out. "I appreciate your help in securing it."

"Tiamat is being ridiculous," Kishar said. "She must know Abbi always buys more than we could possibly use in one household."

"Still, I am grateful," Rahab said. She did not know what she would do if she could not feed her guests the salty cheese and fresh milk. She handed her sister the coins to pay for them, and Kishar slipped the money in her pocket.

"And this is from Mama," Kishar said, handing Rahab a bag of boiled milk sweets and some dried fruit. "She says there will be more soon."

"Thank you." Rahab took the treats and placed them in her bag too. Mama always tried to send little things when she could, as long as Father was not aware.

Rahab leaned in to hug her sister before turning back to her home to prepare for the night's guests. Perhaps, if she was careful with her coins, soon she would be able to save enough to pay down her tax bill, and she could breathe a little easier. She just needed to welcome a few more guests. She hoped the night would bring some more travelers to her inn.

CHAPTER FOUR

It was nearing nightfall two weeks later when there was a knock at the door. Both of her guests were already in for the night. Hazi was back, along with another guest, Nirgal, a trader in metals, who was resting upstairs. She left the pot of lentils boiling over the fire and opened the door to find two men she did not know standing at the top of the steps.

"We are told this is the best place to stay for a night in Jericho," said the taller one. His dark hair was long, his beard neatly trimmed, his skin smooth, and his features even and pleasing. He was smiling, his eyes kind. He was handsome, striking, but there was also a sense of gentleness in his demeanor.

"I am afraid I cannot claim that honor," Rahab said, looking from the handsome one to the other, who was shorter but much more solidly built. "But I can offer you a safe place to sleep and a warm meal."

She could not make out where these men were from. They spoke with an accent that said her language was not their first, and yet they spoke it well. They did not have the weary, road-worn look of so many of the travelers who appeared at her door, though their traveling cloaks and dusty feet and sandals said these men had been on the road.

"That is all we require," said the stockier one. "Do you have space?"

"You are welcome here," she said, stepping back. She named the price for one night's stay, and they agreed it was fair. "You may tie up your animals in the area just below there. There is an extra charge for feed and water for them, but they will be safe here."

"Thank you," the taller one said. "We have a cart as well, full of valuable goods. May we bring the goods with us?"

"Of course," she said. "They will be safe inside."

The shorter one nodded.

"Where are you traveling from?" Rahab asked, trying to place the accent.

"We come from Hebron," the taller one said. "Do you know it?"

Rahab knew of Hebron. It was a large city on the main trading road, and very prosperous. The hills around the city were said to be ripe with grapes, from which some of the finest wines were made. Rahab had hosted many traders from Hebron. But these men did not sound like the guests she had met from that area. No matter. They were surely not the first men to obscure their origins on the road. As long as they had the money to pay for their lodging, she did not much care where they came from.

"I am Rahab," she said, looking from one to the other and letting her eyes rest perhaps a second too long on the face of the tall one. "Welcome."

"Salmon," said the handsome one, nodding. "It is a pleasure to meet you, Rahab." He met her eye, holding her gaze, and she felt something stir inside her. He was handsome, true, but there was something else there, something revealed in the kindness of his eyes, in the set of his mouth, that Rahab wanted to learn more about. But she forced herself to look away and at the other man.

"Ronen," he said, nodding. His hair was shorter, cut close to the scalp, but his beard was longer, and thick. "We are pleased to meet you."

"Come inside." She led them inside and into to the main room, where the pot of lentils still boiled over the fire. A loaf of bread cooled on the table near the stove, its sweet scent mixing with the onions and herbs that cooked with the lentils. The serving table was cleared, the room neat, as it was before meals. Hazi reclined by the window, drinking a cup of wine, and he looked up as Rahab led the men into the room.

"Hazi, these are Ronen and Salmon," she said, gesturing at the new guests. "This is Hazi. He is from Beersheba, but he stays here often."

Hazi nodded at the men and then turned back to his wine. Rahab led the men up the steps to the level with the sleeping rooms. The two rooms for guests were on either side of the stairs, and her room was at the end of the small landing.

"Hazi and Nirgal will be in here." She indicated the room to the left of the stairs. The deep rumble of snoring within told her that Nirgal was resting before dinner. "But you may use

31

this room." She opened the door to the right and showed them the space. It was small, barely large enough for two grown men to stretch out on the mat on the floor, but the window gave a good view of the spring and the trees beyond.

"It suits our needs perfectly," Salmon said, once again giving her his kind smile.

"You may set your things down in here, in that case," Rahab said. "Supper will be served shortly." The men thanked her, and she retreated down the stairs to finish preparing the meal. The two men went downstairs to take care of their donkeys and unload their cart. As soon as they had gone, Hazi spoke from his seat by the window.

"Where are they from, then?" Hazi nodded to the door, where the men had disappeared.

"They told me Hebron." Rahab set the bread on a dish and carried it toward the table.

"They are not from Hebron," Hazi said, shaking his head. "What is their business?"

"I did not ask." Rahab was curious as well, but there would be time to ask them while they ate.

Hazi looked up at her from under his heavy eyebrows.

"What is it?" Rahab drizzled golden oil into a pool on another small dish.

"You do not know who these men are. They could be anyone. And yet you let them in."

"I run an inn, Hazi." She carried the dish to the serving table and set it beside the bread. "It is my business to let in people I do not know. As long as they pay me, I do not ask questions."

"In normal times, I can understand that," Hazi said. "But these are not normal times."

Rahab put her hands on her hips and studied him. "You are still worried about the Hebrews."

"As should you be. I have heard more about them. They used to be slaves in Egypt, until their god sent terrible plagues over the land and Pharaoh was forced to set them free."

"I do not feel bad for the Egyptian king for losing his slaves."

"Then their god dried up the Red Sea, and they marched across on dry land. Pharaoh's army followed, pursuing them, but as soon as the last Israelite had stepped out of the sea, the waters returned, drowning the army behind them."

Rahab had no time for such nonsense. "You should not listen to such stories. You know that is impossible."

"And yet they did. Their god made it so."

Rahab laughed. "In that case, I would like to meet this god."

"Perhaps you will. Perhaps we all will, if they march here next."

She heard footsteps on the stairs. The men were coming back up.

"Do you see an army?" Rahab gestured out the window. "Surely they would have brought an army with them, if they intended to take Jericho."

Hazi gave her a long, appraising gaze. "They could be spies, you know."

Spies again. Everyone in this town was becoming paranoid. She hoped rumors such as these would not keep visitors from Jericho.

"As could you."

"You know I—"

Hazi fell silent as the door opened, and Salmon and Ronen entered the room once again. Rahab's eyes went to Salmon, as if drawn by some force, and when he met her eyes, something passed between them. An understanding, somehow—almost as if he saw her in a way that no one had in a long time. She felt a warmth spread through her, and something about the way he looked at her let her know he felt it too.

Behind her, she heard Hazi gasp. She reluctantly pulled her eyes away from Salmon's to see what had disturbed him. That was when she noticed for the first time what they had brought into her home.

Both men's arms were piled with rich linens, fabrics woven into intricate patterns with thread dyed the most beautiful crimson and deep indigos and shot through with gold. Rahab had never seen one cloth hold so many colors in it. She had never seen cloth woven into a pattern like that. She'd heard that such richness existed. Father had even bragged of seeing fabric like this once. King Uz's first bride had worn a gown made of the finest silk from Damascus, a city known for its textiles, at their wedding feast. He'd talked for weeks about the way the cloth shimmered and the colors woven into it seemed to come alive.

How had this man come into possession of so much of this precious cloth? The bundles in their arms must have cost a fortune. More than Rahab saw in many years.

From the corner of her eye, Rahab saw that Hazi's mouth hung open.

"We will just leave our things in our room, and then we will be back down for the meal," Ronen said.

"Of course." Rahab had not known they intended to leave a small fortune in their room. She would have—well, there was not much she could have done, she knew. She would just have to make sure their things stayed safe. Hazi would not disturb them, she hoped. Nirgal did not know they had brought such riches into the inn. She hoped he would not find out.

When they had gone up the stairs, Hazi turned to Rahab. "See? They are thieves."

"You do not know that."

"Who but a thief could have riches like that?" Hazi hissed.

"Perhaps a king." Rahab did not know who else would have such finery.

"A king. Have you ever seen a king ride into town on a donkey? With no fanfare, no attendants, no soldiers? A king, checking into the inn run by—"

"It is unlikely." Rahab cut him off. She did not need to be reminded why hers was the cheapest inn in Jericho. "But if not a king or thieves, I do not know how they could have finery like that."

"We are not thieves, nor a king."

Both Rahab and Hazi whipped around, and Rahab saw that Ronen and Salmon had come back into the room. How had they come so quietly? But they must have heard what Rahab and Hazi had said. It was Ronen who had spoken, but both wore smiles on their faces.

"My apologies, sirs," Rahab said quickly, bowing her head. "We did not mean to offend."

"No offense is taken," Salmon said, and walked forward. "But I assure you, you have nothing to fear from us."

"We are linen traders," Ronen said. "Come to do business with the palace."

Rahab quickly poured each of them a cup of wine and held them out to them. As Salmon took the cup from her hands, his fingers brushed against hers, and she felt a spark, as from a flame, shoot through her. She forced her fingers to pull away, and both men took their cups, and Rahab gestured that they should take a seat at the dining table. Salmon sat on the wooden bench on one side, Ronen the other.

Hazi had stood from his seat by the window and made his way over to the table. He took the seat next to Ronen. He looked very small next to Ronen's broad shoulders and thick arms. Indeed, the wooden beams that held up the ceiling seemed lower than before now that they were in the room.

"That must be some serious trading," Hazi said, taking a big gulp of wine. He held out his cup for more.

"We have had good fortune in our business ventures," Salmon said.

Rahab retrieved the big jug and refilled his glass just as the stairs began to rattle. A moment later Nirgal appeared in the doorway, summoned from his nap by the sound of voices, and Rahab gestured toward the table.

"Nirgal, our new guests are Ronen and Salmon." She nodded at each man. "They trade in fabrics. They are here for business with the palace."

Even as she said the words, she realized how strange they sounded. Most who did business with the palace stayed there, or at least at one of the better inns nearby. Why were these men here?

"Who are you meeting with there?" Hazi asked. "I have sold some of my leather to the artisans who created the king's clothing."

"I cannot recall the name of the man at the palace we met today," Ronen said, scrunching up his brow. "Though I am sure it will come to me."

"Is it Jazeer?" Hazi asked.

"Yes, that is right," Salmon said. "Jazeer asked us to meet him in the morning."

Hazi tilted his head. "Jazeer is a woman."

"Of course," Ronen said quickly. "That is right. She is."

"We met with many in the city today," Salmon added. "We had a great many meetings."

"They are traders from Hebron," Rahab said, trying to rescue them from the awkward moment.

"Ah, Hebron. I have spent much time in Hebron," Nirgal said, settling onto the bench next to Salmon. "It is a wonderful city. Have you visited the palace gardens?"

"Oh yes," Salmon said quickly. "The gardens are beautiful, especially when the flowers are in bloom."

"I have always enjoyed my time in that city," Nirgal said. "There is a stand where they make the best roast goat I have ever eaten. Have you had it?"

"The food here smells wonderful," Ronen said, turning toward Rahab. She understood he meant that they were hungry, so she quickly served bowls of the lentil stew topped with cooked onions, and the men helped themselves to the bread and cheese on the table.

All four of the men dug into their bowls heartily. Salmon asked Nirgal about his business, and Nirgal was happy to tell him about the market for rare metals. Rahab watched the interaction from her spot by the fire. She always tried to remain invisible during meals. Her guests thought of her as a servant, nothing more. Tonight, Rahab listened with interest though. It had not escaped her notice that the newcomer had not answered Nirgal's question about the food in Hebron. But surely that did not mean anything. Ronen had known about the garden. They had just been hungry. And, in fact, Ronen had already finished his stew. Rahab hurried to refill his bowl and Salmon's too, and both men quickly ate.

"It is wonderful stew," Salmon said, looking at her again. She looked away.

"I am glad you like it." She moved back behind the cooking table. "It is just a simple stew."

"We have not eaten anything like it in a long time," Ronan added. "One gets sick of bread."

"The bread in Hebron is wonderful too," Nirgal said, and told them about another merchant in the market, who sold pillowy yeasted loaves. The men nodded, but did not add to Nirgal's comments. Salmon glanced over at Rahab a few times, but she pretended not to notice, somehow managing to pull her eyes away just before he caught her admiring his form.

Ronen then asked Hazi about his business, and they spoke about the tannery his son now ran, and how far his business travels took him, and soon Hazi was speaking about a recent journey through the plains of Moab, turning the conversation to the topic that seemed to be on everyone's mind.

"Have you heard of these infidels who call themselves the Israelites?" Hazi asked.

"We have heard of them on our travels," Salmon confirmed. "It is said their army is very powerful."

"Unbeatable," Ronen added, using a crust of the bread to scrape the last of the stew from the bottom of his bowl. "At least, that is the rumor, after they defeated the king of Bashan."

"I have it on good authority that the rumors are false," Nirgal said, shaking his head. "I was told today that they have not defeated Og after all."

"I am afraid your source is wrong." Salmon stated it so simply that for a minute, Nirgal didn't seem to know how to respond.

"Og is dead," Ronen confirmed. Quickly, he added, "At least, that is what I am told."

"But they are mere nomads," Nirgal said. The derision in his voice was clear. "It is impossible. How could a small tribe of nobodies have defeated the most powerful king in the region?"

"It is said it is because of their god," Salmon said. "The god they worship, Yahweh, is said to be more powerful than all the other gods. I have heard that it is Yahweh who has brought them victory."

Rahab watched him speak, her mind whirling. He spoke with such authority that she found herself inclined to believe him. But how could he know such things?

"That is what is said in the market, at any rate." Salmon shrugged and popped the last of his bread into his mouth.

Ronen stood. "I am very tired. I fear we must go up before I fall asleep at this table."

"That is a good idea," Salmon said, standing beside his friend. He lifted his bowl and began to carry it toward Rahab.

"Please, leave them on the table," Rahab insisted. What were they thinking? Guests did not usually offer to help. "I will clean up."

"Thank you for a wonderful meal," Salmon said. Was she imagining it, or did he let his gaze linger a moment longer than necessary before he turned and followed Ronen up the stairs?

CHAPTER FIVE

Once the two new visitors were upstairs, Hazi and Nirgal began speaking about the Israelites again, arguing once more over their might. They did not seem to have picked up on the strangeness of the men's exit, how quickly they seemed to want to be gone after Salmon spoke about the Israelite god.

The light in the window began to fade as evening advanced. Rahab lit a lamp before setting it on the cooking table, and she used a jug of water to clean off the dishes as she puzzled over what she had seen. Salmon and Ronen said they were from Hebron, but they did not seem to know much about the town. They were in possession of vast riches, including cloth that only came from the east. She thought Damascus was not so far from Bashan, the area that was rumored to have been taken by the Israelites from King Og. A king whose demise Ronen had been quick to confirm. The two men said they were traders, and yet they seemed to not know the person at the palace they were supposed to meet.

Could it be... But it was impossible.

Still...

Was it possible that these men were the spies Munzur had warned her about?

That was silly, though. These men were nothing like the warriors the Israelites would have sent. Not only that, these men would make terrible spies. Spies were meant to go unnoticed, to blend in, weren't they? But who could fail to notice Salmon's striking looks? He could never blend in or go unnoticed. It made no sense.

Rahab finished cleaning up while Hazi and Nirgal continued to argue. Eventually, they grew tired of sparring and went upstairs. Rahab wiped off the table and was about to go down to feed the animals before locking up for the night when a knock sounded on the door.

That was odd. The city gates had been closed some time ago. Was someone looking for lodging at this hour? Rahab carried the lamp over and opened the door cautiously.

"Yes?"

A man stood at the door, his face shadowed by his hood. In the dim light from the lamp she could see that he was tall and wiry, with pale skin marked by disease.

"I am looking for a room," the man said. "I was told this was the right place."

"Come in," Rahab said, stepping back to let him inside. "You will have to share a room, and the meal has already been served, but there is space."

She closed the door behind him and held up the lamp. She could see him more clearly in here. His dark hair was lank and knotted, his teeth mostly rotten. But it was the way that he looked at her that unnerved her the most.

"You are as beautiful as they said," he said, moving his gaze over her body. "I am pleased."

"Payment is due up-front," Rahab said. She took a small step back from him. "You can store your animals in the small area under the house."

He did not move, just continued to smile at her. It was deeply disturbing, the way he was looking at her. It was almost as if he thought—

"How long do I get?" he asked. "Do you charge by the hour or by the night?"

"This is an inn, sir. You must pay for the whole night."

"An inn." He winked at her. "Of course. The whole night then." He rubbed his hands together. "That is very good."

"Sir, I am not sure what you—"

"We shall have a lot of fun." He reached into his robes and pulled out coins, which he set on the table, and then he stepped forward and grabbed her wrist. "Can we go somewhere a little more private?" He pulled her toward him, and Rahab yelped as pain shot through her wrist.

"I am afraid you must leave," she said, trying to keep her voice steady. She tried to pull her arm away, but he held her firmly in his grip. "This is not that kind of establishment."

"They said you were the prettiest little harlot in town, and look at that, they were right."

She tried to push him away, but he was much bigger than she was. She struggled to get away from his grasp, but he pressed his body against her, pulling her toward him, and started to put his hands all over her.

"I am not a harlot. You must stop. I—"

He covered her mouth with his, and though she tried to scream, she barely made a sound. His hands were working on the cord at her waist that tied her robes together, trying to untie the knot. Her heart pounded in her chest, and her head was starting to swim. She could not breathe. Yet she pushed against him, kicked at him, but that only seemed to make him more eager. She screamed again, scratched at his face with her nails, but he—

Suddenly, the man was pulled back, yanked off of her, and a moment later landed with a sickening thud on the far side of the room. It took a moment for her to understand what had happened. Salmon was standing before her, fists curled, gazing at the man with loathing.

"Get off her." Salmon's voice was deep, husky, but startlingly calm. Rahab reached for the table, grabbed on to it to hold herself up. Her legs were shaking, and her whole body felt weak.

The man scrambled to get up off the stone floor. "Who are you to tell me to get off of her? I have paid my fee. This harlot is mine for the night." He pushed himself up to his hands and knees and struggled to stand.

"She is no harlot."

Rahab sucked in long breaths, trying to steady herself. Shame flooded her at his confidence. Rahab wanted to disappear into the floor. If only he knew about her past, he might not be so quick to defend her.

"She is known as Rahab the harlot, is she not?" The man had pushed himself to standing now, but he stayed where he was.

"Get out." Salmon said it so coolly, so calmly, that it was almost chilling. The man took note of the tone as well. He looked from Rahab to Salmon and back again. For a moment, Rahab though Salmon was going to strike the man in the face. But then the man seemed to come to some sort of decision.

"I will take my money back."

In response, Salmon grabbed the man by the collar and shoved him toward the door. He yanked the door open with one hand and tossed the man out onto the top step with the other. The man landed hard on the ground. Salmon grabbed the coins he'd left on the table and threw them out after him, hitting him in the face and back, before slamming the door shut. He quickly took the big wooden beam and threaded it through the loops to secure the door, and then he turned back to Rahab.

"Are you hurt?" He gazed at her not with disgust, but with compassion.

"No," she said. "I do not think so."

"I am glad." Salmon stepped toward her but hesitated, as if unsure what to do.

"Thank you." She meant so much more, but this was all she could find the words to say.

"That man was vile."

She nodded, trying to get her mind to work. There was so much she wanted to say, but she could make herself say none of it.

Salmon watched her for a moment, and then he said, "You must sit." Softly, he put his hands on her shoulders, and when she did not shrink at his touch, he guided her to the table. She allowed him to help her sit on the bench, and then he walked back toward the serving area and took two clean cups. He grabbed the jug of wine and poured the dark liquid into the cups, set the wine back on the shelf, and carried them back to the table.

Rahab watched, confused. Men did not serve themselves, but waited for women to bring them what they required. And yet he acted as if there was nothing odd about this at all. Perhaps things were different where he came from. Wherever that was.

He set the cups down on the table and then took a seat on the bench next to her.

"Are you sure he did not hurt you?" He turned his face toward her. The flickering light from the oil lamp cast dancing shadows over his features, but even in the dimness, his face was kind.

"Thanks to you, he did not." Her arm was a little sore, but she could live with that. "I am grateful for your help."

"I only wish I had hit the man in the face before I threw him into the street." He took a sip of his wine, cradling the cup with both hands. "It must be difficult, running an inn on your own, as a woman. With no one to protect you, I mean."

"It is usually all right," she said. "Though sometimes men get the wrong idea. They assume that a woman running an inn must be running a whole different kind of business altogether."

He nodded. "Forgive me, but I have rarely heard of a woman running an inn on her own. How did this come to be?"

Rahab took in a long breath, and then she let it out slowly. "The place belonged to my husband, before he passed."

"I am sorry."

"Do not be. He was—it was not a love match."

He looked at her, as if trying to understand the things she did not say.

"You did not go home to your family, after he was gone?" Salmon did not look like he was judging her. He truly seemed as though he was trying to understand. And it was no doubt difficult to make sense of, she knew. Her situation was unusual. She tried to figure out how to explain, where to even start.

"My father used to be a very high-ranking adviser to the king," she said. Salmon tilted his head slightly. This was no doubt what he was expecting her to say, so she hurried on. "This was the previous king, King Urbarra. Our current king— King Uz—it was his father. King Urbarra trusted my father, as did his son Utultar, who was the heir to the throne. We had a very comfortable life. My older brothers and sisters married well, obtaining good positions in society. But then Uz challenged his father and killed him, and he drove his brother Utultar out of Jericho, usurping the throne."

It had been a shocking turn of events, but Salmon did not seem shocked. Perhaps this was the way of the world, then, as Gibil had said when he promptly took a position in the new king's cabinet.

"The new king immediately fired all of his father's advisers. My family's fortunes were changed overnight. While my brothers and sisters had all married well, I was still a child, just about to be of marriageable age. My father suddenly had no work, and few wanted to be associated with a man who had supported the old king, for fear of reprisal from the new one. So there was no money for a dowry."

She did not know why she was telling him this. She had rarely shared this part of her life. Not only that, she did not understand why he was sitting here listening to her. Asking her questions as if he honestly cared about the answers. It was unnerving. And yet she found that she did not want him to leave.

"I imagine you must have had many suitors, despite that," Salmon said. "A woman like you?"

Rahab looked down at the table. The grain was fine and had become smooth with use over the years. She could not help but think about Minesh, about his quiet spirit and his gentle touch. Yes, she had had many suitors but only one who mattered. Salmon's statement hung in the air.

"I do not think you understand how things like this work in Jericho," she finally said. "Without a dowry, a good marriage was impossible."

"Men in this city must be blind."

"I suppose there was also the fact that none of them wanted to insult the king."

"How would marrying a beautiful, kind woman insult the king?" He cocked his head.

"He…approached my brother Gibil and offered me a place at the palace."

"The king asked you to be his wife?"

"No." Her fingers found a rough spot on the wood and picked at it. "Not as a wife." A wife would have been a much greater honor indeed.

"I see. Your king has a harem, then?"

Rahab nodded. "It is considered an honor to join the king's household."

"So why did you not take the opportunity? Most would, I imagine. You would have had a comfortable life at the palace. Plenty to eat and drink. Children, in due time."

"Gibil said no."

"Your brother turned down your opportunity to be among the household of the king?"

"Gibil...does not always think beyond what is good for him."

"Why would it not be good for him to have a sister in the bed of the king?"

Rahab picked at a sharp splinter in the wood. "He could not abide the idea that I would be closer to the king than he was, from what I understand. He did not tell me his thinking, of course. But that is what my sister Kishar said."

"And your father?"

"Did not know until afterward. He was very angry. He does not speak to Gibil to this day."

"So instead of becoming a member of the king's household, you were married to an innkeeper, the only man who would have you without a dowry?"

Rahab nodded. She had come to accept this as her lot over the years, and it was gratifying to see Salmon so upset on her behalf. She had been treated poorly. It was evident for all to see.

"The king saw it as a snub, I am told. So even if a man had been willing to go without the dowry, none dared risk upsetting him by marrying me. None but Mashda."

"Was he kind to you?"

Rahab looked up. Was he kind to her? Who was this man, who asked about such things? "It was not a bad life."

He lifted his cup, took another sip, and then set it down carefully on the wood. The coals in the fireplace settled, and crickets chirped in the warm night air.

"And what of your brothers and sisters?" he asked. "You have said they made good matches. Did they not offer to help?"

"Two of my brothers run the iron forge together," she said. "Nuesh and Sagma. They mostly make swords and armor for the king's guard. They offered a small amount but said they needed money for the business. My brother Gibil quickly found a position in the cabinet of the new king, but he said that he could not help or his job would be in danger."

"Your brother once again put his position over the welfare of his sister."

Rahab shrugged. She had long ago come to terms with Gibil's actions. "He had his own family to care for by that time. I imagine he must have been thinking to provide well for them."

"But would it not have raised his honor, to have his sister marry well?"

Rahab did not know what to say. She did not disagree with Salmon. But Gibil had always put himself and his desires first.

"How many sisters do you have?"

"Two. Kishar and Ri. Kishar would have helped if she could. She helps me now, securing things in the market that I cannot. But my sisters do not control the money. They are at the mercy of their husbands."

"And their husbands would not help their wife's sister?" His voice was low. It was clear he was upset on her behalf. She could not think of the last time someone had been upset on her behalf.

She shrugged. "With no dowry, my father's choices were quite limited."

"Did you wish to be married to an innkeeper?"

At first Rahab did not even understand the question. Why was he asking such a thing? "It does not matter what women want," she finally said. "Mashda was older, his children grown. His wife had passed many years before. He was...he was willing, which is all my father truly considered."

"Have you any children?"

She shook her head sadly. "Just one, but he was born too early."

"I am sorry."

He was sorry? This man was strange indeed, to care about her pain. "Thank you," she finally managed to say. She took another sip of the wine to steady herself. "And yourself?"

"Oh no." Salmon shook his head. "No children."

"No wife?"

"No wife."

"Why not?" Rahab could not believe she'd said the words. She had been too bold. Surely he would tell her she had overstepped.

But he did not. Instead, he seemed to consider the question and then finally said, "I suppose it is not my time yet."

Now that Rahab's breathing had returned to a normal pace and her mind was able to focus more, she realized that it was just the two of them in this mostly dark room. She should not be here alone with him. If anyone caught them, they would assume exactly what that other man had. She should go upstairs and go to bed. And yet she found she could not. Somehow, in this moment, it was almost as if they were the only ones in the world, and the regular rules did not matter. Rahab did not want to push too far. But she did want to know more. "What do you mean?"

"I have work to do before I take a wife," Salmon continued. "Important work." He shifted on the bench, turning so he was facing her. "Soon things will be different, and I will be in a position to find a wife and start a family."

"What will be different?"

He lifted the cup to his lips and smiled at her over the rim. "Everything."

What did that mean? "Everything?" His gaze was kind. She should not risk upsetting him with questions. Yet he seemed to want to talk to her. "Is there a big change coming to Hebron?" she ventured.

He set his cup down, a soft smile on his face. "How it is that you managed to keep the inn, after your husband passed?"

She watched him for a moment. He had not answered her question. Now she was even more curious. He not telling her something.

"Where are you really from?" she asked.

"In most cities"—he continued as if he hadn't heard her—"a woman would not be allowed to hold on to the property that belonged to her husband. And yet here you are."

Rahab was not deterred. She could play the same game he did. "I see many guests come and go, and yet I have never seen anyone bring the riches you brought into this inn tonight," she said. "Where did you get them?"

"You have not only held on to your husband's property, you are allowed to stay here, with so many strange men coming and going." Salmon kept his eyes on her, but instead of making her nervous, it made her feel like he genuinely cared. "It makes no sense."

"What is your real business in Jericho?" she tried again.

"There are some in town who say you are running a brothel, you know," he said. "Some in town say that you are a woman of the night, and yet you are so clearly not that."

The words stung. It was as if she'd been slapped. "If that is why you came here, I am sorry to disappoint you."

"That is not why we came here," he said, his eyes meeting hers. "I can see you are a woman of virtue." In the soft light of the lamp, she could see flecks of gold in his eyes. "You are a woman who can be trusted."

He was speaking in riddles. He was saying kind things—things no one had said of her in a very long time—and yet he was not being forthright. She had answered his questions. Now it was time for him to do the same.

"In that case, trust me with the truth." She leaned forward. "Who are you, really?"

He watched her, a smile still playing on his lips. He had not found her questions impertinent. He had not responded in anger. He simply reached for the jug of wine and poured more into his cup.

Rahab was growing more certain her suspicion from earlier was right. That this man was one of the Israelites—a spy sent to scout out the city, to see how best to take it. If she was right, she should be angry. She should throw this man and his friend out immediately. Warn him what they did to traitors around here. About the might of their king's army.

But she did not. If what they said was true—if this man's god truly was the most powerful of all gods—well, she wanted to know more about this god.

"Tell me about Yahweh," she said.

His eyes widened, and in that instant, she knew she was right. This knowledge made her bold.

"Did Yahweh truly dry up the waters of the Red Sea so your people could walk out of Egypt? That is what they are saying, and everyone is afraid. But I want to know. Did He truly help you defeat the kingdoms of Sihon and Og? Is Yahweh truly more powerful than all the other gods?"

Salmon did not answer. He did not seem to know how to respond, but his silence made her more certain that she was right. He was an Israelite spy, sent here to get the scope of Jericho. And yet he did not appear to want her killed for what she had discovered. In truth, he seemed more like he was considering how to answer. Like he wanted to tell her what he knew.

And then, slowly, quietly, he spoke. "Yahweh is not the most powerful god." He took a long, slow sip of his wine and set the cup down gently before he continued. "He is the one true God."

The confession hung in the air, heavy. He waited to see what she would do with this information. She could have him arrested, they both knew, for what he had just revealed. She could rush out now and tell the king's guards. There would be nowhere for the spies to run. The city gates were closed, and they would be found and captured. Rahab would be richly rewarded.

But Rahab wasn't thinking about having the spies arrested. She was thinking about what kind of god this Yahweh must be. How powerful He must be, to have control even over the waves and the sea. None of the gods Rahab knew could do so much. How mighty He was, if He could bring victory to His people, even against the most powerful kingdoms in the world. How He cared for His people, to lead them out of slavery and into a good land. He did not behave like any of the gods she had ever heard of before. She wanted to know more about Yahweh.

But just then, a heavy knock pounded on the door.

"Open up!" a deep voice called. "Open this door by order of the king."

CHAPTER SIX

Rahab looked from the door back to Salmon. His face had drained of color, and his eyes were wide.

"Open this door!" Heavy fists pounded on the door.

They had found the spies.

She stood, her legs shaky. She needed to open the door. She could not ignore the order from the king.

And yet she did not move toward the door. Opening that door would mean certain death for Salmon and Ronen. They would be tortured and then publicly executed. It would be terrible. Would she be arrested with them? She had not known who they were when she let them in. Would the guards believe her?

She looked back at Salmon. If he truly was an Israelite…if he truly was here to spy out the land…his people no doubt planned to do here exactly what they had done to the kingdoms of Sihon and Og. It was horrific. Salmon, as kind as he was, was a representative from an invading army. They were no doubt planning to invade Jericho and vanquish the city, just as they had done at Heshbon and Bashan. She could not protect such men.

Salmon was pushing himself up now. She must act quickly.

"Open this door." The guard outside was getting more agitated now. His fists struck the door with heavy blows. "We know the spies are inside!"

What if she did turn them over? What if King Uz did execute these men? Would that stop the Israelites?

She suspected it would not. They would send more men, more spies. They would still attack the city but with even more vengeance. If Yahweh was who Salmon said He was, He would not be stopped. He would bring victory to His people despite her actions. The Israelites and their god were coming for Jericho, one way or another. The question was, whose side would she be on when they came?

Rahab did not really make a decision—she simply found herself moving. First, she set their cups on the shelf so no one would see two had been here, and then she grabbed the lamp and moved quickly toward the stairs, ushering Salmon to follow her. Without a word, he fell in line with her, and they rushed up the steps, him following just a step behind.

"To the roof," she hissed under her breath. Salmon stopped at the door of the room he shared with Ronen and woke his friend, while Rahab went to the ladder that sat against the back wall. Carrying the lamp in one hand, she climbed the ladder and pushed against the hatch in the ceiling, but it did not budge. She tried again. It did not move. She looked up, trying to see in the darkness what was keeping the door in place. It could not stick now. She must get it open.

Ronen and Salmon came rushing out of the room and toward the ladder. Ronen's eyes were bleary, but he was moving quickly. Salmon carried the stack of linens in his arms.

"It's stuck!" Rahab whispered. She pointed at the square in the ceiling.

Below her, the guards pounded on the doors once again, growing more insistent.

Ronen gestured for her to move aside, so she climbed down off the ladder and Ronen scrambled up. He used his shoulder, bracing his huge girth against the door, and pushed up against the square in the ceiling. With a groan, it gave way. Ronen scrambled up the ladder, Rahab just a step behind, and then Salmon came carrying the pile of riches from their room. When they emerged onto the roof, she gestured toward the bundle of flax stalks she had drying. Moonlight bathed the whole city in pale light.

"Lie down. I will cover you."

She was lucky none of the neighbors were on their roofs at the moment. Her roof adjoined the ones on either side, the houses pressed right up against one another. Tonight, there was no one to see what she was about to do. Both men lay down on the roof, and she untied the rope that held the flax stalks together and piled the stalks over the top of them. It was not perfect, but they would be hidden from view. "Do not move," she said, and as quickly as she could she scrambled down the ladder and replaced the door and then hurried down the stairs. Hazi, awakened by the noise, was on the first floor, walking toward the door.

Rahab stepped into the room, knotting her robe tight around her, and yawned. She set the lamp on the table. "What is that noise?" She shook her head, trying with all her might to act as though the pounding had just woken her from a deep sleep.

"Guards," Hazi said. "They say they are looking for spies."

"Spies?" Rahab rushed to the door, and Hazi helped her remove the beam that bolted it shut. Then she pulled the door open and blinked against the bright light of the torches on either side of her door. Two guards stood on the top step. Behind them, guards trailed down the steps, swords drawn.

"What took you so long?" The guard standing directly in front of the door wore the full metal armor of the king's guard. It was Abu-Waqar. Kishar's husband. His eyes showed no recognition of her and no hint of kindness.

"I have just woken up," Rahab said. "I was in a deep sleep. What is the meaning of this?"

She could not tell how many there were, but there looked to be at least a dozen men outside her door, each wearing a metal breastplate emblazoned with the red falcon, the symbol of the king. She recognized her old friend Minesh among the crowd. She and Minesh had played together as children and had developed feelings much more adult as they grew, but after her father lost his position, she had given up all hope of a match with the handsome neighbor boy. They had continued to meet in secret for some time until she'd been married off to Mashda. She had not spoken to him in some time. He did not meet her eye now.

"There are spies in your house," Abu-Waqar said. "Bring them out, now."

"Spies?" Rahab blinked, trying with everything she had to come across as ignorant. "There are spies here?"

"I knew that was what they must be," cried Hazi from behind her. "I said it, did I not?"

Rahab ignored him and focused on the guards. "Spies?" She made her eyes wide and round, trying for innocence. "Surely not."

"Bring out the two men who arrived today. They are spies, sent to spy out the whole land," said Abu-Waqar. "Bring them to us by order of the king."

"I had no idea they were spies." She shook her head. She sounded like an imbecile. And yet she knew they expected nothing more from her, a woman, and it was buying her time to think, so she kept up the act. "How could that be?"

"They are here!" Hazi said. "I will get them and bring them to you." He was already starting toward the stairs.

She could strangle Hazi for his helpfulness. She would need to play along.

"They *were* here," Rahab said, thinking quickly. She needed to keep these guards from searching her house. "And they were horrible men." She pulled her robe tighter around her. "Thankfully, they are gone now."

"They went up after dinner," Hazi insisted. "Surely they are still here?"

"They are not," Rahab said. She must make Hazi be quiet. "They did go up after dinner. But then, after you went up, Hazi, they came back down, shortly before dusk, just as the gates were about to close for the night. The men left this house. I do not know where, but you should hurry—if you go now, you may catch them."

"Why would they leave?" Abu-Waqar's voice boomed. "Why would they come here and then not stay for the night?"

Rahab thought quickly. The only excuse that came to Rahab's mind was one she definitely did not want to utter. But it was the only excuse she could think of that would likely work.

"They were under the impression that this was a house of ill repute," Rahab said as calmly as she could. "They wanted... more than I was willing to offer."

She could see that her brother-in-law believed it. That everyone in the city knew of her reputation. That even if she did not do the same kind of work as she once did from desperation, the stain of her past still hung over her. It was easy to see how the spies could have believed she was a harlot, she knew. It was a mistake that had already been made once that night. And now, she was grateful to see, the guards accepted her answer.

"But when I told the men that I could not provide what they wanted, they left," Rahab said.

"We should go now and search the city," the guard next to Abu-Waqar said. "We may still be able to find them."

"We must search the house first," Abu-Waqar said, and began to step toward the door. Rahab for a moment thought she might try stop them, that maybe she could block the door and insist they stay outside, but Abu-Waqar did not wait for her to step out of the way before he pushed his way inside. She was forced to step back, and a moment later the guards streamed in, one after another. Metal scraped against metal as they each ducked inside the door. She gasped as the torches were carried inside. One brushed against the low ceiling. If they lit the place on fire, all would be lost—not only the men hidden on the roof but her whole life. This inn was all she had left. But she held her tongue, knowing the guards did not care what she had to say.

She caught the eye of Minesh, the only man she had ever truly loved. He looked away quickly. Whatever feelings had been there were gone now. He followed the guards headed directly for the stairs, while others looked around the main floor. Their heavy steps thudded above, and the ceiling shook. She followed them up the steps quickly, trying her best to keep her breathing slow and controlled. She could not show fear. She could not let them see that she was worried. If the men were found hiding in her inn—if it came out that she had lied to the guards—she would be killed alongside the spies. But she could not let them see on her face that there was any reason for concern.

Rahab reached the second floor and found two of the guards searching the room where the men had stayed. One guard held a torch dangerously close to the ceiling, and another was overturning everything inside the room. They knocked aside the bedrolls, tossed the pot on its side, and overturned the blankets, finding nothing, no sign that the men had ever been here at all. Across the hallway, Nirgal was yelling. It would have been a particularly unpleasant way to wake up, Rahab thought, to find several of the king's armed men hovering over you. She heard the sounds of the night bowl breaking and the thud as the sleeping rolls were overturned in that room as well.

Rahab stepped farther down the small landing so she could see into her own room, where more guards were flinging her blankets apart. She watched as Abu-Waqar stabbed at her bedroll with a sharp blade, puncturing it in several places.

"Abu-Waqar!" Rahab could not stop herself from crying out. "You are ruining it."

"We must make sure they are not hiding anywhere," her brother-in-law said, keeping his face carefully turned away from her own.

"No one could be hiding in my bedroll," she said. "Please stop causing damage for no reason. I beg of you to stop. I told you, they are not here."

Abu-Waqar did stop stabbing her mattress, but he did not apologize for the needless damage he had caused, nor did he refrain from turning over the basket that held her spare robe and other things a woman needed. They fell on the floor before Abu-Waqar tossed the basket next to them and stepped on them as he walked out of the room.

"Up here," another one of the men was saying, gesturing toward the ladder. "We must check the roof."

Oh no. Rahab felt her legs weaken. Not the roof. They could not go up there. "There is nothing to see on the roof," she said, but they moved ahead as if she had not spoken. The largest one, the one who had been next to Abu-Waqar at her door, climbed up the ladder and pushed the door open as if it were made of parchment.

Rahab stood frozen. She did not know what to do. All the guards had to do was to toss aside a few stalks of dried flax and the men would be found. Rahab's chest pounded, and she could not breathe.

If You are real, Yahweh, now is the time to show Your power, Rahab thought. She felt silly. You did not talk to gods as if they were in the same room as you. As if you were their equal. As if they cared about your requests. You knelt before them, you made offerings, you worshiped them. But this was all she had. If Yahweh was real, she hoped He would forgive her. *If You are as powerful as they say You are, Yahweh, close the eyes of the guards. Protect Your servants Salmon and Ronen.*

Another guard climbed up the ladder behind the leader, and Rahab scrambled up behind them. Pale moonlight cast a silver glow over the scene.

"There is nothing here," the first was saying. He held out the torch, turning to take in the far corners of the roof.

"I told you, they are gone," Rahab said. The spies were not two arms' lengths from her. She silently begged them to stay still. "There is no one here. The spies left out the city gate."

"Nothing." The second guard had also looked around the small roof and found nothing. Neither one shone his light in the direction of the flax stalks.

"If you hurry and go after the men now, you may be able to catch them," Rahab said.

"They're not here," Abu-Waqar finally agreed.

Rahab could not believe it. Were they really not going to look? How could these men, who had overturned a small basket of her underthings to search for the spies, not think to look in the only place the spies could possibly be hidden?

Suddenly she understood. Yahweh was protecting His servants.

"Let's go," Abu-Waqar finally said, cursing. He began to climb down the ladder's steps. Rahab held her breath as he went, hoping he would not set the roof on fire with his torch, and then waited while the other man went down after him. Alone on the roof, Rahab wanted to say something to the men hidden below the stalks, but did not dare. She could not put them all at risk now. She climbed down the ladder without a word and found the guards gathering again on the ground floor. The armed warriors made the space feel small and very crowded, and the odor of their bodies was foul. Metal swords scraped against the floor as they moved.

"Where were they headed when they left?" Abu-Waqar called when she stepped into the room. Hazi and Nirgal were seated by the window, and she saw that they had helped themselves to more wine.

"I do not know," Rahab said. "Though I would guess they took the road that leads to the fords of the Jordan River. You may still catch them."

"Let us go," the leader said. "We shall not wait for daybreak. We will get the guards to lower the gates, and we will go after them now."

Rahab saw fear and confusion on the faces of a few of the men. It was not safe to go beyond the city gates after dark. The wilderness was vast and dangerous. But Abu-Waqar had spoken. The king wanted the spies caught.

"We will leave two men outside your door, in case they have not left the city after all," Abu-Waqar said. "If they try to return, our men will catch them."

Rahab supposed she was meant to be thankful, so she nodded and pressed her lips together. There would be guards outside the home. How would she get these men out of here with guards at her door?

Suddenly, all the guards were on their way out the door once again, with no word of apology or acknowledgment of the chaos they had created in her home. Several of the guards kicked at the carts stored under the house, checking to make sure the men were not inside. Rahab let out a long breath. She could not believe they had not thought to ask who the donkeys and carts belonged to. Surely if they had looked closely they would have seen there were more donkeys than guests here. Yahweh must have protected them once again.

When the last guard was gone, Rahab set the bar over the door once again, hoping there would be no more interruptions this night.

Not long after, she heard the groan of the city gate lowering and then the sound of footsteps against the packed dirt of the road. Hazi and Nirgal had gone back up to their room, hoping to salvage some rest this night, but Rahab sat by the window and watched as the king's guards marched away. The men grew smaller as they traveled down the road, and as they walked, Rahab thought over everything that had happened this night. She thought on the strange arrival of the spies. Of the lies they had told about who they were and where they came from. How she had seen through them but somehow not been afraid. She remembered how Salmon had come to her defense and shown her great kindness, how after he'd thrown the bad man out into the street he'd sat with her and spoken to her as if he cared what she had to say. As if he saw her for who she truly was. And she thought about how she had understood who they were, and who they served. The god who had brought them out of Egypt, who had dried up the Red Sea for them, and even, this very night, protected these men from capture.

The guards' torches slowly dwindled as they went down the road, growing smaller and smaller until she could not see them any longer.

Then she silently made her way back to the roof.

CHAPTER SEVEN

When Rahab arrived back on the roof once again, everything looked exactly as it had when the guards had come up not long before. The pile of flax stalks still lay in the corner, somehow undisturbed.

"Salmon?" she called softly. "Ronen?"

"They are gone?" It was Ronen, she thought.

"Shh. Yes, they are gone. I told them you had escaped out the gates, and they have gone after you, down the old trading road. But there are guards at the door. It is safe to come out, but you must stay quiet." She could see the glow from the torches of the guards at her door, chasing away the shadows in the street below.

The flax stalks rustled and began to shift, and slowly their forms emerged. Salmon pushed himself up, and then Ronen stood beside him. Both men brushed seeds and bits of dried husks from their robes. The pile of valuable linens was now covered in a fine layer of dust. Both men brushed off their robes, but they left the fabrics in a messy stack on the ground.

"Thank you," Ronen started to say, but Rahab cut him off.

"I know that Yahweh has given this land to you," she said, and then, taking in a deep breath, she plunged ahead.

"Everyone in Jericho is quaking with fear, because we have heard how He dried up the waters of the Red Sea to lead you out of Egypt. We have heard how He gave you victory over the Amorites, completely destroying the kingdoms of Sihon and Og. Everyone is terrified of you and what you represent. They are afraid because it is clear that your God Yahweh is the true God in heaven and on earth below."

Ronen's eyes widened—with fear or surprise, she did not know—but it was Salmon's gaze that Rahab sought. He was watching her, and there was something in his gaze she could not read.

"When you come back to take Jericho for your own—" She could not believe she was saying the words. It was horrible. Unthinkable. And yet there was no doubt in her mind that that was what would happen. "When you take this city as the land Yahweh has given you, please show kindness to my family."

"We will," Ronen said. "You will be spared."

He did not deny the plan, then. He did not deny that they would need sparing. She supposed they were far beyond the point of pretending now.

"Swear to it," she said. "Swear an oath that you will spare the lives of my father and mother, my brothers and sisters, and their families. All who belong to them. Swear that you will protect them from death when you take Jericho."

"We swear to it," Salmon said.

"Your lives for our lives," Ronen added. "If you do not tell anyone what we are up to, you will be spared. We will treat you kindly and faithfully when Yahweh gives us this land."

"I will tell no one," Rahab promised. "But how will you know? You know me, but you do not know my parents and those in my family. You must give me a way to signal who you must spare."

Neither man spoke for a moment. Ronen looked at Salmon, who pressed his lips together and looked around. Then his eyes alighted on the pile of cloth at his feet.

"Take this," Salmon said, picking up a braided cord made of fine silk thread. The cord was woven of many strands into a thick rope, and it was dyed, she could see in the moonlight, a deep shade of scarlet. This much fine silk would be worth many months' wages on its own, but the deep crimson dye was costly and difficult to make. This braided cord was worth a fortune, but Ronen barely glanced at it as he handed it to her. These men did not understand the value of the fabrics they carried with them. They did not understand, or they did not care, Rahab realized. "Tie it outside your window. Gather your family into your house. We will spare all who are inside the house with the red cord."

Tie the cord and leave it hanging outside the window? It was not unusual for those living against the wall to hang fabric from their windows to dry. But she had never heard of a cord hanging from a window for any length of time. "Surely they will wonder why I have hung this cord. What will I say?"

"You may say whatever you like. Only do not remove the cord, or all will be lost," said Salmon.

He held out the red cord, and she reached to take it from him. As her fingers brushed against his, he did not pull his hand away. Indeed, he let it linger, touching her fingers with his, threading them through his own, before he finally pulled them away. She dropped her hand quickly, taking the cord, wrapping its length around her elbow.

"You must understand that we will not be able to control the army once they have started to invade," Ronen said. It was clear he had not noticed that anything out of the ordinary had just happened. Had she imagined it altogether? "So make sure everyone you love is in the room with the red cord. If anyone is out on the street or elsewhere in the city, they will not be spared. Do you understand?"

"I understand," Rahab said.

"But if anyone is inside the home with the red cord, we will not touch them. If we do, their blood will be on our hands," Ronen said. "And if you tell anyone at all—even a single soul—the deal is off."

"I understand," Rahab repeated. So many feelings pressed up inside of her. Relief that she and her family would be spared. Fear that something would go wrong and they would be killed, along with the rest of the city. Disgust and utter horror at what these men were preparing to do.

But also, somewhere beneath it all, an incredible peace. It felt as though her heart was quiet and calm, her spirit content, for the first time in many years. Yahweh was the one true God, and the knowledge quieted her deepest fears and her long-buried disappointments. None of that mattered now that she knew the truth.

"Now you must go," she continued, gesturing for them to follow her down the ladder. "Go to the hills." She pointed in the direction where the sun rose. There was nothing but a vast black expanse now, but they nodded. "There are many caves in those hills. The wilderness is vast, and there will be good places to hide. Go there, and hide out for a while, until the king's guards realize they have lost you and come home defeated. Then you will be safe to go on your way."

"The hills are to the west?" Ronen was squinting into the darkness.

"They are that way." She gestured with her arm. "Now go, before the other guests find you here. The door is being guarded, so you will need to go out the window." She picked up the rope that had kept her flax stalks bound. "We can use this, and I will lower you down."

"Are there guards stationed around the city walls?" Salmon gestured toward the corner of the city, where a tall stone tower rose, lit by the glow of a torch inside. If the guard looked this way, he might be able to see the men escape out the window.

"Usually they only stay in the rooms at the corners. Let us hope they are all distracted by the excitement at the city gate," Rahab said.

"It is dark enough that if we are quiet, they may not notice us," Ronen said. Rahab hoped he was right. The moon cast enough light that she could see them well enough now. But she supposed it was their only hope. "Let us pray that the Lord will close the eyes of the guards."

"We must ask Yahweh for protection," Salmon said. "Let us go."

Rahab started toward the door, and Salmon followed a step behind, Ronen just behind him, but suddenly Rahab stopped. "You are forgetting your linens."

"We must leave them behind," Ronen said quickly. "They will only slow us down, and speed is of the utmost importance."

"But—" He could not be serious. "You must take them. They are worth far too much to leave behind."

"Take them yourself," Salmon said. "The cart and donkey too. As our way of saying thank you for protecting us tonight."

"I cannot." What would she do with linen so fine? "They are far too precious."

Ronen was already reaching for the door in the floor, but she was in his way.

"Perhaps you can use them to make something nice for yourself," Salmon said, but he was distracted, focused on getting away safely. If it had not been so ridiculous, Rahab would have laughed. She could hardly show up at the market wearing a robe of Damascus silk, dyed in colors fit only for royalty. People would think she was a thief. Or, more likely, that she had begun selling herself again, and had found a very wealthy patron for her trouble. They would call her a harlot, and worse. "Or sell them. We do not care. They were nothing but a cover for us. They are yours to do with what you wish."

"Only do not forget to hang that scarlet cord from your window when you see our army coming," Ronen said.

"I will tie it there now." Rahab still did not know what to make of their strange gift, but she would think about that later. For now, she needed to focus, as they were, on getting them safely out of Jericho before they were caught. She stepped aside, and Ronen opened the door and began to carefully climb down, taking care to stay as quiet as possible. Salmon followed, and then Rahab, and she led them into the main room. They walked toward the open window and Rahab looked for somewhere to tie the rope they would use for escaping.

"This," Ronen said, pointing to the metal loop that allowed the shutters to close. He quickly tied the rope through the bracket and pulled against it to test the knot's strength.

"It will hold," Salmon said. He gestured for Ronen to go first, and Ronen hiked his leg over the edge of the window and grasped the rope in both hands. Rahab leaned over and gazed out at the ground below. It would be a long way to fall. But Ronen nodded, steeling himself, and began to climb slowly down the rope, bracing his feet against the city wall but holding with all his strength to the rope. When the rope came to an end, still a good way from the ground, he let go and landed softly on his feet on the hard ground. She heard no noise from the guard tower.

"Your turn," Rahab said to Salmon, who nodded and stepped toward the window. But before he grasped the rope, he turned back to Rahab.

"We will not forget you." He reached out his hand, nearly touching her wrist. She ached to move closer, to feel his fingers on her skin, but she stood still, and he dropped it again. "I will not forget you, Rahab."

Then he took the rope, slung his leg over the windowsill, and quickly climbed out the window and lowered himself. Rahab stepped forward and watched as he dropped the last few feet to the ground, landing with a soft thud. In the milky moonlight, she saw them turn in the direction of the wilderness and run toward the hills. She quickly pulled up the rope and untied it, and she watched until they vanished around the side of the city wall, and even then she kept gazing out at the dark night.

Her body ached with exhaustion, but her mind was not quiet. She replayed the events of the night over and over in her mind, trying to make sense of all that had happened from the moment the strange guests had arrived at her inn. They were Israelites, spies sent to scope out the land they would conquer. They would fight King Uz's army, but they would win, because they served the one true God, who was giving them this land. They would take Jericho, and when they did, she and her family would be saved. But only if she did not tell a soul what was coming.

Could she really do it? Could she really keep quiet about what she knew? It was treason, not telling the king what she knew. But more than that, it was wrong. Rahab did not know how she could go out in the morning and talk with Munzur, go to the market and laugh with Mostafa, and not tell them to prepare themselves, to flee the city, to find safety somewhere else if they wanted to live. How could she not warn them? How could she go on as if everything were normal when she knew the bloodshed that was to come? And yet if she did, she knew all would be lost. A heavy weight sat upon her chest. Did it make her as bad as the Israelites if she kept quiet?

Then again, were the Israelites truly bad? Ronen had not seemed evil. Salmon was kind and caring and had protected her. And if their god truly was giving them this land, did it still make them malicious invaders? Or did it make them rightful heirs, come to reclaim their kingdom? She thought of King Uz and of his brother Utultar, who had been the rightful heir. If Utultar came back to Jericho now to claim his throne, would she feel he was wrong to claim what was rightly his?

Rahab took the scarlet cord from the table and tied it into the iron loop at the base of the shutters. She would do what the men had asked her to do. She draped the cord out the window, where it fell back against the rough stone of the city wall. The fine thread would be ruined, but she found she did not care as she once would have. All she could do was wonder whether it would be enough. Whether this piece of thread would really protect them all. Would the Israelites do what they had promised? She hoped she could trust them. She hoped she could trust their god. She hoped she had not just made a terrible mistake.

Rahab closed the shutters, blocking out the world outside of the city gates. She did not know what would happen. All she knew for sure was that everything had changed this night.

CHAPTER EIGHT

W hile Rahab prepared the meal the next morning, she willed herself to keep her hands and voice steady. She needed to act as though nothing was different, as if she knew only what Hazi and Nirgal knew about the men who had stayed at her home last night. But she could think of nothing else.

Rahab had brought the fabrics Salmon and Ronen had left behind into her room, hiding them as best she could inside the basket that held her spare robe and other things. She had puzzled over what to do with them. Salmon had told her to keep them, but she had no use for such fine cloth. She might be able to sell them. The money she would get from their purchase would pay off her taxes, and she would have plenty left over. She would be free of Penzer, at least for a little while. But how could she sell them? Where would she do such a thing? And what would be the point? If she was right, Penzer would not be alive much longer anyway. She gagged as she thought it. She did not like Penzer, but she got no joy imagining his death. In any case, she could not simply turn up at the market with rich fabrics that were far too fine for her. It would be obvious that she had gotten them some illicit way. It would not be safe. Rahab puzzled over what to do and kept the fabric well hidden.

Rahab did not make her traditional offering to Yarikh that day. The little statue had lost all of its power. It was just carved wood. Yarikh had never given her much beyond a few pennies here and there. The previous night, she had seen what a truly powerful god could do.

As her guests ate their morning meal, they spoke of nothing except the spies the king's guard sought.

"To think, they were here, right next to us," Nirgal said, shaking his head. "How did we not know?"

"It is not a surprise to me," Hazi said. "I knew something was off about them. I told you, Rahab, did I not? I thought they had to be either thieves or spies."

"You did say that," Rahab said from her position by the stove.

"You did not believe me, but look, I was right," Hazi said, triumphantly.

"You were indeed." Rahab did her best to keep her voice level.

"Where could they have gone, once they left this place?" Nirgal asked. Hazi thought they had fled to scout out Jerusalem next, while Nirgal thought they would head west, toward Aphek and Joppa.

Rahab hoped that they had made it to the wilderness safely and found a good place to hide in the hills.

Two guards were still stationed outside her door when Rahab went out. They gave her wary looks but stepped aside so she could go down the steps. Rahab walked through the streets, past the noisy neighbors and the abandoned house, and toward the gates. When Rahab approached Munzur, he told her how the guards had lowered the gate late at night and rushed off in search of the spies. "I told them they were wasting their time, that no spies had gone out the gate before it closed, but did they listen to me? Of course they did not listen to me. I see who comes in and who goes out all day long, but they think I do not know what I am talking about. They do not pay me any mind."

For once, Rahab was glad no one gave any credence to the words of the beggar at the city gates. There was nothing wrong with his mind, only his body, but that did not stop most people from underestimating him.

When she got to the market, news of the spies was on the lips of everyone there as well.

"Can you believe they were here, in this very city?" Mostafa, the vegetable seller asked.

"Surely they are planning an attack," Haran, the man who sold dried meat, said. "We must be ready."

"It is said the men escaped from your inn," said Shenbar. Rahab startled. The man never spoke to her, but it seemed this morning things had changed. "How could you have let the spies escape?"

So she was now being blamed for the spies' escape. Well, she supposed Shenbar was right about that. It was due to her that the Israelites had gotten away. But she could not let them know the truth.

"If you had summoned the guards sooner, they would not have escaped," added Haran. "Why did you not sound the alarm?"

"I did not know they were spies," Rahab said.

"How could you have not known?" Shenbar asked. "Evil men like that, they could not simply blend in like normal people. You must have known."

Rahab did not bother defending herself. She wanted to shout that they were spies, that it was their job to blend in, that though they had spoken to many in the city the day before, none had recognized them for what they were except Rahab. But she did not. She kept quiet, ducked her head, and tried not to think of what would happen to all of these people when the Israelites did come back to Jericho with their army. She did her shopping, and then she began her true task of the day.

The home where Rahab had grown up was not far from Kishar's house, along a wide street shaded with palms. The houses were larger here, freestanding, and many were filled with fine things. Rahab's father had possessed quite a fortune at one time, though now the house revealed several places where the limestone facade was in need of repair, and she knew the roof leaked in wet weather.

Rahab took a deep breath, steeled herself, and knocked on the wooden door. She had not been to this house in quite some time. Had not been welcome inside for longer.

The door was pulled back, and Rahab's mother stood there in the narrow doorway. There had not been servants for years, so Rahab was not surprised to see her, but she was startled by her mother's appearance. She had grown thinner, her hair grayer, than when Rahab had seen her last.

"Hello, Daughter," her mother said, her eyes crinkling at the corners as she smiled. "You are looking well."

"Mama, I must speak with you. May I come inside?"

"You know that is not possible, child." She said it sadly, and Rahab knew it was not her mother's choice that barred Rahab from entering the family home. Mama had always shown her youngest daughter kindnesses whenever she could. It was Rahab's father who had barred her from entering the home, from interacting with members of the family. It was her father who worried that the stain of her reputation would sully them all.

"Mama, I have something important I must tell you," Rahab said. "Father need not know."

Her mother's eyes searched out her own, and Rahab saw love in them. Mama did wish things were different, Rahab knew that. But a woman could not defy her husband once he had spoken.

"He will know," Mama said. "How are you doing, Rahab? Are you well? Do you have enough to eat?"

"I am well enough, Mama. Thank you for the dried fruit and the sweets. Kishar passed them along to me. They are much appreciated."

"I wish I could do more to help, but you know your father, he will not—"

"I understand, Mama." It was the same whenever Rahab spoke to her mother. Today, she needed Mama to understand something important. "Mama, please listen. I need to tell you something." Rahab had thought through what to say on the walk over here. She could not tell anyone what she knew, but she had to say enough to get them to listen to her. "If the city is in danger, you must come to me."

"What are you talking about?" Mama asked. "What danger?"

Her mother went to the market every day. Had she truly not heard? Then again, Mama had always been good at ignoring the things she did not want to believe.

"All I can tell you is this: If an army marches on Jericho, you will be safe at my home. Only at my home. Come to me, when the time comes."

"You know your father would never enter your home," Mama said. Rahab knew it was true, but the words still stung. Still, she needed her mother to understand the importance of what she was saying.

"You must. When the time comes."

"Whatever for?"

"I cannot say," Rahab said. "Only that you must."

"Omarosa, who is that?" It was Father, calling from inside the home.

"It is no one," Mama called back over her shoulder. "A beggar."

"Well, send her away."

Mama turned back, her face strained. "I am so sorry."

Rahab had long ago learned not to expect her mother to stand up for her, at least not if it meant displeasing Father. But it still hurt. One's mother was meant to love and defend, even when no one else did.

"I will go, but you must promise."

Rahab heard footsteps inside the house. Father was coming to shoo her away, believing her a common beggar. If he saw who was truly at his door, he would send her away even more quickly, believing his youngest daughter to be lower than a beggar.

"I will do my best," Mama said, and then, with an apologetic nod, she quickly closed the door. Rahab wanted to scream. Could not they put aside their concern about propriety to save their skins? Could Mama not bother to try to understand what Rahab was trying to tell her?

"Harlot."

Rahab spun around, but she could not tell which of the neighboring buildings the insult had come from. Someone had called down to her through an open window. Rahab had known all of the neighbors her entire life, played with their children when she was young. This was how they saw her now.

Somewhere deep down inside, she wanted to feel a little bit glad these people would soon be getting punished. They would shortly get what was coming to them. But she could not. It gave her no pleasure that blood would soon run through these streets. In was unthinkable. Rahab turned and hurried down the street and turned the corner, making her way to Kishar's house. She was welcomed inside there, but when she sat with her sister in the courtyard and told her the same thing she had told Mama, Kishar too responded with confusion.

"What do you mean that we must come to your home if an army marches on the city?" Ushi was sitting in a patch of grass and clover, investigating the strings of a palm frond that had fallen to the ground. "Why would we do such a thing? You must come here, if such a thing were to happen. This home is much more secure than where you live, right in the city wall."

"Normally, yes, I would agree with you. But you have to believe me. When the time comes, you must be with me in my home. You and your family and servants."

"Why, Rahab?" Kishar tilted her head. "Why are you telling me to do a thing that makes so little sense?"

"I cannot give you a reason," Rahab said. She thought for a moment. Surely the Israelites would never know if she shared just a tiny bit with her sister. Just enough to get Kishar to believe her. But she had sworn an oath. If she broke it...well, the Israelites might not know, but their God no doubt would. "But please, promise me."

"I cannot promise such a thing," Kishar said, narrowing her eyes. "Unless you can tell me why. And even then... Abu-Waqar will never agree to such a plan."

"Please." Rahab reached for her sister's hand. "And please tell Ri to come as well. She will not hear it from me, but she needs to believe me."

Kishar did not say anything for a moment. She stretched out her legs in front of her on the bench. The sun's rays brought out the fine weave of the fabric of her robes.

"Abu-Waqar was at your home last night, I am told."

"He was one of many armed guards who appeared at my door last night. They searched my home, ruined my things, and upset my guests. And they did not find what they were looking for."

"They were looking for the spies from the Israelite army who were known to be at your home last night."

"But they did not find them."

"People are saying the spies escaped from your inn before the guards could catch them."

"What they are saying is correct," Rahab said. She hated to lie to her sister, but she knew she must. "The men were at my home, but they left shortly before the city gate was raised for the night."

"They are saying in the market that the men left after they had gotten what they came to your place for."

Rahab opened her mouth to speak but closed it again. Kishar was telling her the gossips in the market were accusing her of selling herself again. She would have thought she would be used to it by now—the feelings of shame and embarrassment whenever she heard such things. But the lies hurt afresh, every time.

"They left because they did *not* get what they were hoping for," Rahab said as calmly as she could. Still, she heard her voice shake. "Please make sure to correct any who misunderstand this. The spies had heard in the market that I was offering more than a roof over their heads for the night. When they found out I was not in that business, they left. That is the last I saw of them."

Rahab uttered the lies in a steady voice. It felt wrong to spread lies about Ronen and Salmon. They were her enemy, representatives of an invading army, yet they had been kind to her.

"They are saying you should have known who they were and stopped them."

"How was I to have known?" Rahab asked. There was no way to win against the gossips, she knew that. But it would be

85

better if the lies at least made sense. "They were spies. It was their job to not be noticed."

A light breeze caught the hem of Kishar's robe, and she pulled it down. "Were the men huge, as they are saying? Stronger than a normal man and twice as tall?"

"Surely I would have noticed if that were the case," Rahab said. "They were nothing of the kind. They were just normal men." Salmon's searching gaze flashed through her mind. He was anything but normal. "They said they were textile traders from Hebron. That is all I know about them. They asked for services I do not provide, and they left. That is the last I saw of them."

"Abu-Waqar has gone after them, I am told," Kishar said. "He has not yet come home."

"A large group of guards went after them," Rahab confirmed. "Let us hope they find them and bring them back here to face the king." Rahab hoped nothing of the sort.

Kishar nodded, brushing a hair back behind her ear. "I imagine Gibil is not having a good day." She met Rahab's eye, a smile on her face.

Raba could not help it. She laughed. "No, I imagine he is not. I suspect the king is not happy this day." It was funny to imagine her smug older brother trying to placate the king, assuring him everything was under control when it very much was not under control. "Will you get the message to Gibil as well? About what to do when an army attacks?"

Kishar watched her. "You will not tell him yourself?"

"You know he will not see me."

"It is madness. When he is the one who could have done the most to help. To keep you from—"

"Just please tell him." Rahab pushed herself up. She did not want to hear this again. She knew as well as Kishar did that their oldest brother had the resources to help her, had he chosen to, but he had not. She had been trying to understand how he could now shun her for what she had been forced to do, and it was a struggle. "I must go now."

Kishar nodded, and Rahab bent to kiss Ushi before she made her way to the door.

"Be safe, Rahab," Kishar called. Rahab nodded, puzzling over the comment, before she stepped back out onto the street. The heavy door fell closed behind her.

Rahab thought about what to do next. Ri wouldn't see her. Her sister was far too concerned with her reputation to be seen talking with Rahab. She had made that clear on many occasions. She must trust that Kishar would pass along the message. And Gibil would be at the palace now. His wife Erish also did not want Rahab in their home, so she could not go there to warn the family. But Sagma and Nuesh might see her. Her youngest brothers were busy with their work and families and did not have much time for Rahab, but they were both always kind to her. She made her way back to the western side of town, the less desirable part of the city, where the necessary but unpleasant businesses were allowed to do their work. It was not far from where Rahab's inn was.

Rahab heard the sounds from the foundry before she was close enough to see it. Metal banging on metal. The incessant, ear-splitting pounding of the smith's hammer against bronze as it cooled meant that only the least desirable would choose to live nearby, and the few people she passed on the street did not meet her eye. The doors and windows were wide open, as usual, when Rahab arrived, but the heat and the noise inside the forge was still overwhelming. Rahab found Sagma bent over a workbench, hammering a long, thin piece of glowing metal into the shape of a sword. Toward the rear of the shop, she could see Nuesh working near the blast oven, where the bronze was melted and purified. The flames of the furnace glowed brightly in the dim space. Sagma looked up and smiled as she walked in.

"Hello, Sister," Sagma called. His robe was open to let in as much air as possible, his sleeves rolled up, but he was still sweating through his clothes. After only a few moments in this shop, Rahab was sweating as well. "I have heard you are the most popular woman in Jericho today."

"I do not know that I would say that," Rahab said.

"It is said the spies were at your home." Sagma straightened up, setting down his hammer. "Did you really see them?"

"I did meet them. They just seemed like ordinary men," Rahab said. "And they left before the city gates closed. I am sorry to disappoint the gossips, but I do not know more than that."

"But they were at your home," Sagma said. "You saw them. Is our brother asking for your help in finding them again?" His eyes were wide, his boyish face open.

"I am afraid not," Rahab said. She did not want to talk about this again. "If you hear any more about this, please tell the gossips that I do not know anything about the whereabouts of the evil spies."

"That will never satisfy them," Sagma said, crossing his arms over his chest. "How about I tell them that you recognized them for who they were and sent them away?"

"And threatened to kill them if they ever came anywhere near Jericho again?" Nuesh had stepped closer without Rahab noticing. How had he overheard them over the roar of the furnace? Yet he joined the conversation seamlessly. Those two had shared a womb and had always seemed to be able to know whatever the other knew.

Rahab laughed. "That would be some story, but sadly, it is not the truth."

"But you did recognize them by their pointy teeth and horns, right?" Sagma asked. He raised his eyebrows and smiled. "That is what they are saying about them in the streets."

"And for their incredible strength?" Nuesh added.

"Sadly, they were just normal men," Rahab said. She knew her brothers were only teasing, but did some people truly believe such things? "You would not recognize them as any different from any other man."

"Well, that is disappointing," Nuesh said. "That will never do in the marketplace."

"We will need to repeat the story about their teeth and horns," Sagma said. "That is a much better story."

"That will bring us notoriety among fools, which is all we have ever wanted," Nuesh said, a smile on his face. "Now, Sister, what brings you to our fine establishment this day? I assume it is not to order a set of armor or a sword for yourself?"

All the armor in the world would not prepare them for what was coming, Rahab thought.

"Not today." Rahab tried to sound lighthearted, though she was anything but. "I came to give you a message. It is one that will not make much sense at first."

"In that case, we are the right people to hear it," Nuesh said.

"When a foreign army comes to fight us, you must come to my home," Rahab said. "You and your families. You will be safe there."

"What do you mean, we should come to you when a foreign army comes?" The joking tone had left Sagma's voice. "Do you know something after all, Rahab?"

"You have heard something from the spies," Nuesh said.

"No, no." Rahab had said too much. She could not betray her oath. "Truly."

"You are lying to us," Nuesh said. "The only way your message makes any sense is if you know something you learned from the spies."

"Go on, then." Sagma crossed his arms over his chest. "Tell us."

"All I can tell you is that if an army comes, you must come to my home. That is the only place you will be safe."

Nuesh and Sagma turned to one another. Sagma's eyes were wide.

"You made a plan with the invaders." There was something like admiration in his voice.

"No, I did not," Rahab said. "Please. You must believe me."

"Oh, sure." Nuesh nodded, but his face showed he did not. "We believe you. We believe that you know nothing about these spies, that you did not recognize them before they left your home. And yet you have a plan for how to keep us safe when their army attacks."

"It sounds completely believable," Sagma added, as if considering it.

"I know nothing," Rahab said. "Tell no one about this conversation. There is much at stake."

"You truly did make a deal with them, did you not?" Nuesh had cocked his head. "Our little sister, the agent for the enemy."

"It is not as you say. I am not—"

"Outsmarting all the king's men," Sagma added.

"Ooh, Gibil is going to be so mad!" Nuesh said. "When he finds out his own sister has helped the spies escape, he is going to go wild."

"And here we are, working on a huge new order of weapons and armor for the king. He is trying to arm every citizen of this town, I think. Against the men you helped escape!"

"This will be so much fun," Sagma added, clapping his hands.

"It is not as you say," Rahab said sternly. She had to make them stop. What if someone overheard? "What you are talking of is treason."

Her brothers looked at one another again, and then back at her. "It is only treason if you get caught," Nuesh said.

It was blasphemy. They could all be killed over the words.

"Do not worry, sister." Sagma smiled at her. The half-hammered sword before him had gone cold, its tip a plain grayish brown, though the flames behind Sagma still raged in the fireplace. "Your secret is safe with us."

"And now that we know you're in league with the enemy, you can be sure we will come to you if the Israelites attack," Nuesh said.

Rahab hesitated. This conversation had gone completely out of control. She was not to have told anyone what she knew. Then again, she hadn't told them. They had guessed. But would it matter? She had made a solemn pact.

"I deny everything," Rahab said. "Only, come and bring your families and, Mama and Father, and all of our brothers and sisters. Please."

"When will it be?" The joking tone had gone out of Sagma's voice. "When will they come to attempt to take our city?"

"I do not know," Rahab confessed. "Just that when they do, it will be swift, and they will not lose."

There was a moment of silence as her brothers absorbed this.

"We can bring our families? Servants as well?" Nuesh asked. He too had seemed to understand the gravity of what Rahab was saying. He had a new baby at home, a son. Rahab guessed he was thinking of him.

"Bring everyone who belongs to you. Just do not fail to come."

Sagma nodded. "We do not understand how you managed it, Sister, but you have always been the most clever of any of us.

You would not risk everything to say such things unless you were sure."

The relief she felt at being believed mixed with the terror at having said too much.

"We will be there," Nuesh said.

CHAPTER NINE

It was two days later that she heard the scrape of metal against metal and many heavy footsteps coming down the street outside her home. She knew who was at her door before the heavy knock sounded. Rahab set down the dough she was kneading and made her way to the door. She took a deep breath before she pulled the heavy bar out of the brackets and opened the door.

There had to be two dozen men in the narrow street. There were more soldiers than she would have guessed, but she was not surprised to see them. She had expected them. What she hadn't counted on was seeing her oldest brother standing before her.

"Gibil." He was tall, and he had grown thicker around the belly since she had seen him last. He wore a fine linen robe trimmed in gold, and his hair and beard were oiled. Working so closely to the king had treated her brother well. Behind him stood several other men in robes—Rahab recognized them as further advisers to the king—the army behind them. From the neighboring windows, several faces were observing this show of the king's might.

"Rahab." He did not duck his head to acknowledge her. He did not even look at her, but kept his chin up. "We are here to find out what truly happened the night the spies escaped."

"What truly happened?" The guards must not have found Salmon and Ronen, then. These men would not be here if they had found the spies. She felt a flush of relief, just beneath the dread that began to rise. Had Sagma and Nuesh shared what they had guessed? "What do you mean?"

"We want to know what happened when the spies were here," Gibil said. "And we want the truth."

Rahab pressed her lips together. She could not tell them the truth, no matter what happened.

"Would you like to come inside, brother?" Rahab held the door open. "We are disturbing the neighbors."

Gibil's top lip curled up. "I would never go in there," he said, straightening his spine.

Rahab was surprised at how much the words stung. Even now, even when he wanted something from her, he would not miss an opportunity to remind her that she was worse than garbage, that he would be soiled by any connection with her. She should not have been taken aback. She should be used to it by now, but his words still hit her like a lash.

Gibil had not always been like this. When they were younger, he had doted on his youngest sister, the baby of the family. He had sneaked her sweets and picked her up when she fell. It was only later, after father had lost his position with the old king and Gibil had secured his position with the new one, that he had begun to turn his heart away from his family.

"In that case, Brother, I will tell you what I have already told the men who were here before. The men came here looking for something I do not provide, and they left disappointed.

I did not see them after that. I do not know where they went, only that they left the city just before the gate was drawn up."

"That is what you told the men the other day," Gibil said, nodding. "But what I am after is the truth."

"That is the truth." Rahab had told the lie so often, even she was starting to believe it.

"The king's men did not find the spies near the river."

"I am sorry they did not," Rahab said. "They were nasty men. Horrible." Even as she said the words, she remembered how Salmon had protected her from the stranger at the door and then sat with her, talking to her as if her thoughts were important. "I want nothing more than to see them captured."

"The guards at the city gate do not recall seeing the spies leave before the gate was drawn up."

"You know better than to trust the word of the guards at the gate. They are as often drunk as not."

"You will not insult members of the king's guard," Gibil said sharply.

Rahab did not move. He knew as well as she did that what she had said was true.

"I do not know what else to say, Brother," Rahab said. "I cannot tell you any more than I have already said."

"You can tell me the truth!" Gibil raised his voice, his frustration getting the best of him. "This is not a game, Rahab. The king is beside himself. He is taking it out on me, demanding answers as to how the spies could have escaped. You must tell me what truly happened that night."

"I have told you all I know," Rahab said calmly.

"You have hung a red cord out your window. It can be seen on the approach to the city, and it appeared the same night the spies escaped. What is the meaning of that?"

Salmon and Ronen had told her to say whatever she needed to. "It is unlike you to take an interest in decorating a home, Gibil."

"It is a message, is it not?"

Rahab laughed. "It is a belt, not a message. If every piece of clothing that was hung from a window in this town was a message, your men would spend much time trying to understand them all."

"You have told our mother and sister to come to your home when the Israelites attack. That is a strange request for someone who knows nothing. You know more than you say."

"My home is secure," Rahab said. "The city wall is solid. In the event of an attack, it is the safest place. You must come too, you and your family."

"You are lying to me." Gibil forced out the words through gritted teeth. "Where are the spies?"

"Your guess is as good as mine, Brother."

"Lying to me is treason."

"Lying to the king is treason." There was steel in her voice. "Do not forget, you are not the king."

"You will be executed if we find you are hiding anything."

"All I am hiding is my disdain for a brother who could treat me as you have."

"I am warning you, Rahab. This is not a joke."

"I do not find it funny myself," Rahab said. "I cannot help you."

With that, she closed the door, blocking out Gibil's shocked face, and she laid the bar across it with shaking hands.

CHAPTER TEN

Two days passed, and then three, and though she was visited once more by a representative of the king's guard, life settled into a normal pattern once again. She cooked and cleaned for guests, went to the market, and visited her sister and mother. She sold the donkey that had belonged to Salmon and Ronen in the market and received a few coins that she would soon turn over to Penzer. She never stopped thinking about Salmon and Ronen, though, or about the promise they had made to her. She never stopped thinking about their God, Yahweh, who she knew to be the one true God. How was she supposed to worship this Yahweh? Did He demand offerings, as all the other gods did? How would she make offerings and sacrifice to appease Him? She did not know. She only hoped He would not forget her. She hoped Salmon would not forget her. She had not forgotten him.

As the days passed, the furor over the spies seemed to slowly die down, and Rahab did not feel as many eyes on her as she had in the days following their visit. And yet with each passing day, she saw more men in suits of armor patrolling the city and standing guard on the towers at the corners of the wall. Rahab continued to serve her guests, continued to visit her sister and mother, continued to hear the whispers about her and see the looks in the street. She held her head high. These people saw her only as the thing she had once been, but that was not who she truly was.

With each passing day, the memories of the night of the spies faded, until she could scarcely believe that it had truly happened. Only the pile of fabrics in her room made her sure she had not imagined the whole thing. Each morning, she looked out her window, where the red cord still hung, watching for movement on the horizon, but there was nothing.

And with each new morning, she wondered anew at the God who Salmon and Ronen served. Rahab wanted to know more about Him. What powers did He have? What sacrifices would He like best? How could she learn more about this God?

Then, after several weeks had passed, word came to Jericho that the Israelites had walked across the Jordan River as if on dry land. Their god had dried up the water for them, it was said. The news was whispered in the marketplace and shared by Rahab's guests. Everyone, it seemed, was terrified that they would march toward Jericho. Rahab bit her tongue to keep from sharing what she knew. But given the news, she was sure Yahweh was as powerful as Salmon and Ronen said.

Though she did not want to, Rahab went to pay Penzer again on the first day of the next week, and she could see as soon as she stepped into his small room that something was different today. Penzer did not meet her eye when she entered, but his mouth curled up in a smug, satisfied smile. That could be the effect of the opium—the scent hung in the air again, and today he had not bothered to hide the pipe he used to smoke the foul substance—but something inside her knew it was more than that.

"Hello, Penzer." Rahab reached into her bag and pulled out her coins. She had had a full inn these past few days, and she was glad to have a bit extra to give him today. "This does not pay off my debt entirely, but it is more than usual." She held the coins out, and though he looked down at them, he did not move to take them.

"It is not nearly enough."

"I understand that," Rahab said. "But it pays down some. And I'm working to get you the rest shortly."

"It is too late," Penzer said. "Your taxes are too great, and your paltry attempts to pay them do nothing but frustrate the king."

"The king knows of my taxes?" Rahab doubted the king paid any attention to things as banal as taxes.

"The king does not like to be cheated."

"I am not trying to cheat the king. I am trying to pay the debt I owe."

"And I am afraid time has run out. The full balance is due by the end of this week, or we will be forced to take possession of your house."

"You will take my house?" Rahab could not believe it. It was all she had. If the king took it, she would not have even a place to live, let alone a way to make money. But that wasn't the most obvious problem. "It does not even belong to me. It belongs to my husband's family."

"It is your husband's debt you are trying to repay, is it not? The money he wasted on opium and the women who sell it?"

Rahab blinked. Penzer never missed a chance to remind her that her husband had not been faithful. To make sure she knew what he had gotten up to at the lounge where he went to smoke. It used to bother her, but she found it did not sting like it used to.

"I cannot lose the house."

"Then you must pay your debt in full by the end of this week." What did the king even want with a poorly built home in an unfashionable part of town? A house built directly into the wall, no less? Only those who had no choice lived in a house such as hers. She doubted anyone associated with the king would choose to live there. It would surely end up sitting empty. This was being done just to punish her.

"How much will it take to pay it off?"

He showed her a sum on the parchment in front of him. It was enormous. It was impossible. She could never get that much money together by the end of the week.

If only her father or her sister would take her in… Maybe she could ask again. If she did not have a place to live, what would she do?

And if they took her home, she would not be able to be in the room with the scarlet cord when the Israelite soldiers advanced. She would be killed, along with everyone she loved. She had to hold on to that house.

If she started selling her body once again, could she raise the amount she needed? She felt bile rise up at the thought. She could never raise enough money in time. Her body was not worth enough to—

But then she realized that she had something in her possession that would pay it all off and more. She immediately felt lighter. All was not yet lost.

"See that you bring it by the end of the week," Penzer said. "I look forward to it."

Rahab did not waste time. After she had done her shopping, she took the folded fabric from the basket in her room and ran her fingers over the top piece, a beautifully woven silk with the distinctive raised pattern that indicated it came from Damascus. She did not know how the weavers managed to make silk do that, to form images with just the thread itself, but it must have taken years of work to weave this one piece. And the colors were stunning—a purple the color of the sky just before night fell fully, a red the color of ripe pomegranate seeds, gold like honey, like the sun on a summer afternoon. The price of the dye alone made this piece the most costly thing Rahab had ever held in her hands. She had heard that the purple dye was only made near the sea, and was made from snails. It took thousands of the creatures to make one drop of the precious dye. And the red dye was made from hundreds of beetles that had been ground up and boiled. Rahab was not sure how it was done, but Ri had told her about it at length when she worked on the robe she wore when she married Hirin. Ri had managed to buy a small amount of red-colored trim, and she had acted as though the small bit of braided cord made her as important as royalty.

The second piece in the stack was a flat-woven red silk. Rahab did not think she had ever felt a fabric as smooth and fine. She could not imagine wearing it against her skin. One would have to be of great importance to wear something as precious as this. And there were four other folded pieces of fabric beneath them, as well as various bits of cord and trims.

For a moment, Rahab wondered about how Salmon and Ronen must have acquired such costly goods. She had already guessed the silk must come from Damascus and that they had gotten it in the east. But to have taken so much of the fine silk... She shuddered to think it. There could have been no one left to care about it. The Israelites must have pillaged the palace of one of the Amorite kings after they took the city and walked away with this and more. These precious fabrics were the spoils of those cities' destruction. She tried to still her heart and steady her quaking hands. That was what they intended to do here in Jericho as well. They planned to take the city and kill everyone inside, and there was nothing she could do to stop it. Their army was too strong. Their god was too strong. She could not stop it, but she could save those she loved. And to do that, she would need to save her home.

Rahab hurriedly tucked the fabrics carefully into the bag she used for the market. They would not all lie flat, but she knew the wrinkles could be steamed out later. The bag was heavy, but she tried her best to carry it close to her body to keep it safe. She walked carefully down the steps and out into the street. People pressed close against her on each side, and she did her best to kept the bundle from getting damaged. She wanted to laugh. If anyone she passed knew what she carried with her now... They would never believe it, though. No one would try to rob her of her parcel, because none would ever dream that someone like Rahab could have something worth taking.

Abbi welcomed her when she opened the door of Kishar's house, and she told Rahab that Kishar was feeding Ushi and Hili was out, but she could wait in the courtyard. Rahab thanked her and took a seat on the familiar bench and set the bundle of fabric down next to her. There was a soft breeze that rustled the palm fronds and spread the sweet scent of jasmine throughout the yard. The breeze also cooled her flushed skin, and as she waited, she felt her breathing slow to a normal pace and her heart stop pounding. By the time Kishar emerged, carrying a squirming Ushi in her arms, Rahab had had time to think about what she would tell her sister about how something so fine had come into her possession.

"Hello, Rahab." Kishar set her son down, and he scampered off to examine a patch of dirt under the palm trees. "How are you this day?" Kishar lowered herself down onto the bench too, the bag of fabrics between them.

Rahab did not have it in her to waste time on pleasantries today. "I have had bad news, unfortunately. Penzer tells me he intends to take my house."

"That toad. He acts as though he is the king himself, feeling himself far too powerful. King Uz does not even know the man's name."

"And yet he can take my home, and he will."

"Oh Rahab." Kishar shook her head. "We must stop this. I will talk to Abu-Waqar again. He cannot let this happen. He will help, I know it."

He had not been willing to help before. Rahab did not know what would make him change his mind now.

"You do not need to ask him. I have—"

"I will get Hili to ask. She is old enough now to understand. And he cannot say no to her. I will—"

"You will not have to ask your husband for money. But I do need help." Rahab opened the top of the bag, and Kishar gasped. "Can you help me sell this fabric?"

"Where did you get that?" Kishar stammered as more of the cloth came into sight.

"I know it is worth a great deal. I believe it will be enough. But I cannot sell it myself."

"Rahab. What have you done?" Kishar was looking at her, the fear in her eyes mixed with amazement.

"I did nothing wrong," Rahab said. "A guest left this with me. A gift."

"A gift." Kishar's eyebrow was raised. "He must have enjoyed his stay quite a lot."

"It is not like that." Even her own sister assumed the worst. "I did not—" She wanted to explain, but she knew she could not. "Please, just trust me. It was a gift. A kind gesture. And now I need your help."

"A kind gesture worth more than this house." Kishar reached out and brushed her fingertips over the surface of the fabric that was on top of the stack. It was the cloth woven in many colors. Despite herself, she smiled just at the touch. "Is it stolen?"

"No." One could not steal from the dead. "It was brought by a trader in fine cloths. He came from the east. He did not steal it."

"And you did not steal it from him?"

"I did not. Like I said, it was a gift."

"You cannot expect me to believe you did nothing wrong to procure such a fine gift."

"You may believe anything you like," Rahab said. "Just help me, please. I need to sell the cloth, for the highest possible price. And I cannot do it myself. Everyone will assume, as you did, that I have done wrong. They will not buy it from me but arrest me, assuming I have taken it."

Kishar lifted up the top fabric and examined the one underneath, the crimson silk.

"Do you know who would be interested in buying such nice cloth?" Rahab asked. "I thought the palace would be the most likely buyer, but do you know of anyone who can get it there?"

"Yes, I think so." Kishar pulled the red silk out of the stack and unfolded it, holding an edge up. It shimmered gently in the breeze. "My friend Inanna has a sister who makes robes for the palace. I think she would be able to help." She lowered the silk and brushed it gently down her arm. "It truly is beautiful. It will look stunning on one of the king's women."

For a moment, Kishar looked her way, something like pity in her eyes. "Do you ever wonder how different things would be if Gibil had not interfered?"

Rahab sighed. Of course she did. She thought about that every day of her life. She could be the one wearing the robes made from these extraordinary cloths. She would know the whisper of fine silk against her skin. She would eat meat every day and have as many sweets as she desired. She would sleep well at night, secure in knowing she would not end up living on the streets if she could not quickly come up with a large sum.

But she could not afford to let herself dwell on what might have been. She must focus on surviving what was right in front of her.

"I do not think red is my color," Rahab said. She tried to make her voice sound jaunty, but it fell flat. "Will your friend's sister pay a fair price?"

"Inanna is very fair," Kishar said. "I am sure her sister is the same." She set the fabric down on the top of the bundle. "But she will want to know—will someone come looking for this fortune?"

"No one will come looking for it," Rahab said. "It was a gift, and mine to do with as I see fit."

Kishar shook her head again. "You are full of surprises, little sister. How long have you had these riches stored up in that inn of yours?"

"Not long." She needed Kishar to understand how dire her situation was. "Please, sell them as quickly as you can. I do not have long."

"Do you think Penzer will really take your home if you do not pay him this week?"

"I do not doubt that Penzer will do exactly as he says. Please, Kishar. This is my only hope."

Kishar nodded. "I will go see Inanna this afternoon."

CHAPTER ELEVEN

Two days later, Kishar was smiling when Rahab appeared at her home.

"Rahab, you would not believe how much those cloths fetched." Kishar pulled out the coin purse that was tied to her belt and began to work on the knot. "I have never seen so much at once in my life."

"You were able to sell them, then?"

"Oh yes. As soon as Inanna saw them, she knew her sister would buy them. She told me when she showed them to her sister, she squealed. She wanted all of them."

"Did she wonder where they came from?"

"I told her Abu-Waqar had won them in a bet at the club. I said the other man was a trader who was not much used to opium. She did not ask too many questions after that. She was so giddy at seeing them that she did not even care. And it turns out, they were worth even more than I thought."

She finally worked the knot out, and she held out the coin purse. "There you go."

It was heavy, Rahab could see that before she took it, but she was still surprised by how heavy it was in her hand. She untied the string and opened the coin purse. She quickly counted what she could see. It was a fortune.

"Will it be enough?" Kishar asked.

"It will be enough," Rahab said. She felt her shoulders relax, and the weight that had been pressing into her chest for days was gone.

"I am glad."

"Thank you, Kishar." Now she would be able to stay in her home. Now she would be there when the Israelites advanced. Now they would all be safe. Kishar had not yet realized that she had saved her own life with this act.

Kishar nodded, still smiling. "I am glad for you, sister. Now go. Pay off that horrible man. Keep your home."

"I will. And when the Israelites come, you must come to the home that you have now helped me save."

"Do not start that again." Kishar waved her hand dismissively. "Just go. I am nervous having that much in my home. Go see Penzer now."

Rahab wanted to argue, but she did not. Instead, she went directly to Penzer's little room in the shadows of the palace and counted out the coins on his desk. His mouth hung open.

"Where did you get all this?"

"That should be enough to pay the entire sum," Rahab said, setting the last of what she owed on his desk. There were still a few coins in the bottom of the purse.

"Who did you steal it from?"

"I'd like to see you mark the account as paid in full, please."

Penzer counted the coins slowly, then counted them again. He tested each one, weighing it out to make sure it was actual bronze. Then, he said again, "Where did you get this much?"

"We can consider my account in good standing, then? And I keep the house."

Penzer looked from the coins to Rahab and back again, and, without a word, nodded.

Rahab turned and walked out of his office as quickly as she could. She hoped she would never have to return. She hoped she would never have to see Penzer's greedy face again.

As Rahab started to thread her way through the crowded streets toward her house, she thought about what had just happened. She was free from the greedy fingers of the king's tax man. The crushing weight she'd carried since Mashda's death had lifted from her shoulders. Maybe now she could save a bit each week. Perhaps she could make improvements to the building and build up a little breathing room.

But then she remembered that Jericho would not stand long enough for any of that to happen. It did not escape her notice that she had the Israelites to thank for her good fortune. The same Israelites who intended to come to the city and destroy everything inside. It was because of this invading army that she had needed so desperately to hold on to her home, or she and her family would be destroyed as well.

As she walked home, the elation she'd felt melted away into dread. She was safe, for now. But what about everyone and everything else?

CHAPTER TWELVE

Two days later, Rahab was awakened by the calling of the king's messengers. She ran to the door and pressed her ear against the wood as the messengers passed through the streets. "All must bring an offering to the temple to lay at the feet of the goddess Ashtart," the messengers called out. They were being ordered to make a sacrifice, then. To the goddess of battle, among other things. The king must be scared. When Rahab went to the window, she saw why.

They were here. They were setting up camp quite a distance away, by the far branch of the river. But there they were. There had to be thousands of them. It had to be the Israelites. She did not know when they would launch their attack, but it could not be long. Rahab checked that the scarlet cord was tied tightly to the metal brace by her window, and then she went to draw water and tried her best to appear calm and serene as she served breakfast to guests who had also been awakened by the calling in the street. She had only two guests this night, Garza and Gishimar. Once they had eaten and set out, she went out with a strong purpose in mind.

First, as always, Rahab went to visit Munzur, and found the city gates drawn.

"What is going on?" Rahab asked the beggar. "Why are the city gates closed?

"The guards are all falling over themselves this morning," Munzur said, taking Rahab's leftover bread from her outstretched hand. "And not just because of drink this time. They could not get the gate closed quickly enough. No one is allowed to go in or out." Munzur stuffed a bite of the bread into his mouth greedily.

"Because of the army," She looked up now and saw that there were more guards than usual in the tower on the wall.

"They have come," Munzur said through a wad of bread.

"The Israelites."

"That's what the guards are saying. They were running around everywhere, in a complete panic. They think I do not hear, but I do. They are terrified." There was something like a smile on his face as he devoured the crust.

"When did the army first appear?"

"Shortly before dawn, marching up the road from the plains of Moab." He put the last of the bread crust into his mouth looked up at her.

"Will the king's army attack them?" Rahab did not know what the king's plan was, but she did know she needed to finish her errands and get back to her rooms quickly. She needed to be in her home, where the scarlet cord hung, when they took the city.

"I do not know. I only know that the guards have been instructed to keep the gate closed. No one is to go in or out of the city."

Rahab thanked Munzur, and then she hurried to her sister's home.

"Kishar, you must come," Rahab said as soon as she saw her sister. She froze. Her sister, always so calm and controlled, was rushing around the room, gathering her things.

Next to her, Hili's eyes were red, and the skin around her eyes was swollen. Kishar carried Ushi on her hip as he played with her gold bangle. "What is it?"

"They have all gone to the armory," Kishar said. "Abu-Waqar and Awil-Ili and Sagar. Gal too." She nodded at Hili, who sniffled. "The king has ordered all able-bodied men to suit up. Have you not heard? The Israelites are coming."

"I have heard," Rahab said. "That is why I am here. You must come with me."

"I cannot come with you," Kishar said. "I must make my sacrifice. Surely you have heard this as well? King Uz has ordered every household make a sacrifice to Ashtart."

"I have heard."

"All are required to make a sacrifice of great value." Kishar tucked the bangle into her pouch. Rahab knew Abu-Waqar had given it to her for their wedding. "What will you give?"

Rahab laughed. "I have nothing of value to give."

"You have nothing left from the sale of the cloth?" Kishar asked.

"Not much." Rahab had a few coins left, but she did not intend to sacrifice them to the goddess.

"You must find something. The king has declared it so," Kishar said. And then, over her shoulder she said, "Come, Hili."

"I do not know what the king could possibly think I have left. His servants have taken everything already."

"I do not know, Rahab. All I know is that Abu-Waqar says King Uz is frightened, and we must comply."

"Do not sacrifice your wedding gold," Rahab said. "Come with me to my home. You will be safe with me."

"I wish that were true, sister." Kishar shook her head. "I wish I could simply hide out with you. But I cannot. I have my children and my husband to consider. I must do as the king has asked. And if you're smart, you will do the same."

With that, Kishar brushed past Rahab and, gesturing for Hili to follow her, rushed out the door. Rahab stood in the open doorway, watching her sister rush down the street. Rahab did not remember ever seeing her so afraid.

And she was right to be scared, Rahab knew. The Israelites were fearsome and powerful. But sacrificing her wedding gold would not protect her from the advancing army. Rahab now knew that sacrifices to the gods were useless, except to Yahweh. Ashtart could not protect them from the Israelites any more than a kitten could. There was no power in the idol the king kept on display in the temple. It was nothing more than a piece of carved ivory. Ashtart was only one of the many gods worshiped in the temple. There was also El, the creator god. Yarikh, the moon god. Ba'al, the god of thunder. There were many others as well, all lined up in the temple, but the only God who could protect them—the only true God—was the One giving power to the army that even now was advancing upon the city.

Back on the street, Rahab could see the king's army gathered on the grounds of the palace, perched high on a hill. The soldiers were milling about in their heavy armor. Rahab supposed the king had put them on display there to calm the citizens, to remind them of the king's power. Nevertheless, the streets were crowded, filled with people rushing about, hurrying to make their preparations. The best they could hope for, Rahab thought, was a short siege. They could hope that the city's walls would stand strong and the king's army would keep the invaders from entering the city at all. The Israelites would likely stand guard around the city, making sure no one could come in or out, hoping to starve them out. But the rumors of what had happened when the Israelites met the Amorites cast doubt on this hope. The Amorites too had strong walls and large armies.

Rahab did not go to the market that morning. She instead went to the home of her parents, to try to persuade them to come with her to her house with the scarlet cord, but no one answered her knock. Perhaps they too were making their sacrifices to Ashtart. She also went to visit her brothers Nuesh and Sagma, asking them to come with her, to bring their brother Gibil and sister Ri.

"We will come as soon as we can," Nuesh said, barely looking up from his work. It was hot in the foundry, and the air was stifling. "First we must finish this order."

"The king has increased the number of weapons and suits of armor he requires," Sagma added. He had dark circles under his eyes, and both had something of a wild look in their eyes. Rahab wondered how long they had been at work.

"The king has ordered that these items must be finished today," Nuesh added.

"But you must come now," Rahab said. "Bring your families." It would not matter what the king ordered for much longer.

"We will come as soon as we can," Sagma promised.

"Please, bring Mama and Father when you do," Rahab said. "And Gibil and Ri and Kishar."

"We will do our best," Nuesh said. "And if things start to look dire, we will leave it all behind and come."

"By then it might be too late," Rahab said. "You will not have time to bring your families."

"For now, they have only set up camp," Sagma said. "There is time yet."

"We will come as soon as we can," Nuesh repeated.

She saw that they would not be persuaded. They still feared King Uz more than they feared the invading army. Rahab returned to her inn empty-handed. The two travelers who had stayed with her last night were now stuck in the city, unable to leave, and she would no doubt be hosting them again this night. She did not have fresh vegetables or cheese to feed them for tonight's meal. Then again, she did not imagine that the city would still be standing by nightfall, so it probably did not matter all that much. Gishimar and Garza, her guests, were out—she did not know where.

From her window, Rahab could see the Israelite army gathering on the flat plain near the river. There were hundreds of them. Thousands. Their bronze helmets glinted in the sun, glowing with a kind of ethereal power. Rahab did not know what they were waiting for. Why did they not simply get this over with? She checked once more to be sure the scarlet cord was firmly tied to the window and sat by the window to wait.

The sun was high in the sky when the Israelite army finally began to march toward Jericho. She heard the noise first, the sound of thousands of footsteps pounding the hard dirt, of metal scraping and jangling with each footstep. But, above it all, she heard—she was not sure. Were those trumpets? Rahab could not see what was making the sound yet, but somewhere behind the thousands of marching soldiers, she thought she heard the sound of trumpets.

"Yahweh, remember me, Your servant," Rahab said quietly. Why were her brothers and sisters not here with her? Why had her mother and father not listened to her? Rahab thought to run out again and insist, but she did not know how quickly the Israelites would take the city. She must be in her home when they did.

The Israelites did not march dozens of men across, as the Amorites had when they tried to take the city years before. Instead, they marched two across, forming a long, narrow line that stretched most of the way to the river. Why were they marching in such a strange and vulnerable formation? She felt a surge of hope. Perhaps this day would not end the way she'd feared.

The men blowing the trumpets were midway through the line, Rahab saw. There were—she squinted and counted as they came into view—there were seven men blowing trumpets, and behind them were four men carrying—what was that? It looked like some kind of wooden box, carried on poles, with two men ahead and two men behind. The men carrying the box were not wearing the same armor as the soldiers. Instead, they were dressed in fine robes made of blue and purple and scarlet yarn. Underneath the robes, they wore linen trousers and a tunic, tied with a sash, all made of the same richly dyed and embroidered fabric. They also wore turbans of the same material, with plates of gold that draped over their foreheads. Rahab did not understand who these men were or what they carried, but it was clear to her that they were important, as they were led by half of the army and followed by the other half.

As the army advanced, Rahab braced herself. Would they attack first? Would the king's army launch an attack from the city walls? She did not know what to expect.

She certainly did not expect what actually happened when the Israelites reached the gates of Jericho.

CHAPTER THIRTEEN

R ahab thought she must be seeing things wrong. She watched through the window while the Israelite army marched in a long line toward the city gates. And then, instead of shooting arrows at the guards on the ramparts, scaling its walls, ramming the city gate to tear it down—instead of any of the things an invading army might do, the Israelites did something that made no sense. They did not fight. They did not rush the city gates, aiming to tear down the thing keeping them from entering. They did not shout or issue a battle cry. In fact, they did not make a sound, save for the trumpets that were still blowing loudly.

Instead, the lead soldiers in the Israelite army turned, and the men calmly began to walk around the outside of the wall. Rahab could not see the men in King Uz's army, but she knew there were men in the guard towers, poised to unleash arrows and spears and all manner of weapons. But no weapons were used. Not yet. Perhaps the king's soldiers were as confused by what they were seeing as Rahab was. Perhaps they were waiting for a signal that had not come. All Rahab knew was that, two by two, the army of the Israelites walked toward Jericho and then turned, continuing to walk in one long unbroken line along the outside of the city wall. Were Salmon and Ronen among them? They must be, but Rahab could not distinguish one man from another. Rahab leaned forward, craning her neck to see what the soldiers at the front of the line would do when they reached the corner, but the lead soldiers had already vanished around the side of the city wall, and still they kept coming. Rahab had never seen anything like it. Did they intend to surround the city entirely? Were there enough of them to make that possible? Was that how they had been so successful against the armies of Sihon and Og? Rahab did not know. All she could do was watch as they continued to come, two by two, marching calmly, silent except for the incessant trumpets.

Rahab did not understand. She pushed herself up and hurried to the ladder that led to the roof. From the rooftop, maybe she could see what they were planning. Rahab grasped the ladder, fingers curled tightly around the rungs, and she pulled herself up hurriedly. She pushed the door up with her shoulder and hurried out onto the roof and toward the edge of the wall. From this vantage, she could see that the soldiers were continuing in their slow march around the city. She could also see guards in the towers at the corners, watching, but holding their fire. Neighbors on several nearby rooftops also stood, watching in consternation as the Israelites made their slow march around the city.

Rahab watched as the trumpeters and the men bearing the wooden box neared the city gate. She wondered if something would happen when they reached it, but they too simply turned and continued to march around the outside of the city. Rahab did not understand what was happening, but she prayed that Yahweh would show mercy.

When the last of the soldiers in the long line had reached the city gates and turned, Rahab braced herself, waiting. But she did not have to wait long, for the first men who had led the army soon appeared around the corner of the wall and marched right back to the city gates before turning and once again marching back in the direction they came, walking back toward the river. Rahab waited for something to change. Was this truly what she had been fearing? *This* was Yahweh's mighty army?

They had not lifted a spear. They had not sent an arrow flying. They had not even attempted to take the city. Why had they not fought?

A sick feeling began to spread throughout her gut. She reached out to hold the wall to steady herself.

The stories of the Israelites' conquest against Sihon and Og must be greatly exaggerated, she realized. Her legs went weak, and she began to see spots in her vision. She realized what that meant. If the Israelites were not the mighty military power they were rumored to be, and if their god had not cleared the way for them to take Jericho, had Rahab made a terrible mistake?

She had betrayed her king and her city, believing these men served the one true God. Because of their might. Because of the obvious power that had given them victory over the Amorite kings. But where was that power today? Where was the awesome display of their God's might? It did not appear to be real today. Had it ever been real at all?

Now, watching as more of the Israelites turned and marched silently back toward their camp, Rahab feared she had chosen terribly poorly. She felt bile rise up in her throat. She had lied to the guards. She had betrayed her brother, her family. She had believed Salmon and Ronen's false promises and their lies. She had honestly thought—

It was too humiliating to even think about now—but for a moment there she had actually believed that Salmon had seen her for something more than a disgraced harlot. She had honestly thought for a minute—

She shook her head. She had been so stupid. That was abundantly clear now. She had sheltered the spies, and they had done exactly what spies did. They had used her, and now that she saw the actual "might" of their miserable army, she knew that she had misjudged terribly. Their god was no more powerful than any other piece of carved ivory. Salmon's attention was nothing more than cunning manipulation. He had done what he needed to do to save his skin, and she had been a fool to believe anything else.

Rahab didn't wait to see the last of the Israelites finish their march around the perimeter of the city. She lifted the hatch and went back inside, wishing she'd never heard of the Israelites.

CHAPTER FOURTEEN

Rahab's two guests had come back to the inn that night full of stories about the day.

"The king has tens of thousands in his army," said Garza, a leather trader who had stayed with Rahab several times on his travels. Rahab doubted this. There were not tens of thousands in all of Jericho. "And they are all highly trained. I saw them gathered outside the palace this day. Those invaders do not stand a chance against King Uz."

Gishimar nodded excitedly. He was on his second bowl of lentil stew and did not seem to mind that she had no fresh vegetables or cheese to serve him.

"Those 'invaders'"—Garza rolled his eyes as he said the word—"have a fearsome reputation that it is now clear they do not deserve. I have never seen an army behave as those fools did today."

"Not one weapon was used!" Gishimar was nearly giddy. His beard was long and neatly trimmed, though he had no hair on the top of his head. He had always proven himself to be an easy guest.

"Perhaps now the guards will open the gates and allow us to leave the city," Garza said. He had not intended to stay in

Jericho for more than one night and had already made muttered complaints about being stuck in the besieged city.

A knock at the door interrupted their banter. Rahab went to the door and opened it, bracing herself. No good had come from answering the door in recent days. But this time, she did not see guards or her brother, just a messenger from the king, who had already moved off to the next house before she got the door open. He was knocking on each door along the narrow street.

"King Uz, in grateful supplication to Ashtart, the goddess of war, who has protected the city this day, demands all citizens make another sacrifice to the goddess of war before sunrise," the man called out as he made his way down the street.

So Uz believed the goddess of war to be responsible for the strange behavior of the Israelites today. Rahab did not know what to think. She had not made the first required sacrifice to Ashtart, because she believed Yahweh to be more powerful. Now she was not sure.

"You must make another sacrifice?" Garza asked when she closed the door and turned back.

"Of course," Gishimar said, dipping the crust of his bread into the remains of the stew in the bowl. "The goddess of war must have protected the city this day."

"What will you bring as a sacrifice?" Garza asked.

"I do not know," Rahab said truthfully. She did not know if she would bring anything at all. How could a carved piece of ivory have caused what had happened today? She did not understand. Was Ashtart really that powerful? Or did none of them hold any power after all? Were all the gods simply stories?

"Well, you had better figure it out soon," Gishimar said as he popped the last crust of bread in his mouth, "if you must make your sacrifice before daybreak."

Rahab nodded, thinking. If the king ordered it, she must. And yet nothing had happened to her when she had not made the required sacrifice this morning. Would the king's men even notice if she did not make a sacrifice?

Rahab pondered this as the men finished their meal and made their way upstairs. Since there were only two of them, they each slept in their own room, a luxury. She cleaned up after the meal and thought about what to do. She had little of value left to sacrifice, even if she had wanted to. The fabric was gone, as was most of the money it had brought her. She had long ago sold the few pieces of jewelry she had. She had nothing left. What could she possibly have to offer?

When Rahab finished wiping the plates and had tidied the table as best she could, she moved to the window. The fires in the Israelite camp glowed orange in the dark night. They were still there. They had not fled the area. Why were they still here? Did they still want to take Jericho?

Rahab reached for the silk cord that hung from her window. She should take it in. It meant nothing now. It was but a mark of her shame for having trusted the spies. She reached the end, where it was tied to the bar by the window and began to untie the knot. It was tied tightly. The soft fibers wrapped against themselves and refused to give up their grip. She worked at it for a moment, and as she did, she realized that the cord itself was worth far more than anything in her household.

If she must make a sacrifice, this would do. She kept working at the knot, and finally got it free. She pulled the cord in and moved to close the shutters when something stopped her. A noise outside the window. But that could not be. She pushed the shutters open again and leaned forward and—

"Rahab."

She shrieked.

"Rahab!" Someone was calling her name from the outside of the wall. Not at the base of the wall but from partway up the wall. It could not be possible, but—

"Toss down the rope."

Rahab leaned out of the window and saw Salmon's face bathed in the milky moonlight. He had climbed part of the way up the outside of the wall, gripping cracks between the stones with his fingers and bracing his foot against the bulging of the uneven stones. It could not be. What was he thinking? Did he want to get them both killed? "What are you doing?"

"Toss me the rope, and I will explain."

She did not know what to do. She could not simply toss him the rope and let him into her home. Even now the guards on the wall were surely watching him. If they saw him climb into her window, she would be executed before daybreak.

But would it be any worse if she did not toss him the rope? Surely they had already seen him. Would the guards believe her, if she claimed she did not know this man? She did not think it possible. Not when they already suspected she'd had something to do with the escape of the Israelite spies.

"Quickly, Rahab."

Either way, his actions now would get them both killed if anyone saw him. And the longer he stayed outside her window shouting for her, the more likely that would be. Rahab reached for the rope, still coiled in the corner of the room, and tied it to the same bar she had just untied the scarlet cord from.

"Here," she called, and lowered the end out to him. He grasped it with one hand, then the other, and, bracing his feet against the wall, managed to pull himself up. Once he had reached the level of her window, he draped his arms over the sill and pulled himself up. Rahab reached for his hand, and she helped him climb inside. Quickly, she pulled the rope back inside and closed the shutters, bolting them securely.

"What are you doing?" she whispered. She didn't want to alert Garza and Gishimar to the fact that they now had a visitor. "Are you trying to get us both killed?"

"Do not worry, the guards did not see me," Salmon said, pulling down the sleeves of his robe. He then calmly brushed the front of his robe off with his hands.

"Do not worry?" She could not believe the nonchalance with which he spoke to her. He was arrogant. He was careless. He had risked her life just by showing up here—not to mention that he was a phony and a traitor and had used her mercilessly.

And yet, despite all of that, she could not deny that a part of her was glad to see him again. Her mind had not kept an accurate picture of how handsome he was, how the angles of his face and his strong jaw made his face difficult to look away from. "How can I not worry when you have just put my life at risk by coming here?"

"I was not seen." Garments fixed, he straightened up.

"How could you not have been seen? There are guards all over the walls of the city."

"Yahweh has closed the eyes of the guards," Salmon said simply. And then, while she was still trying to work out how to respond to that, he continued. "I had to see you. And it is good that I did. What are you thinking, pulling in the scarlet cord?" He bent down and picked up the cord, which lay in a crumpled pile at his feet. "You need to keep this in your window."

A thousand thoughts rushed through Rahab's mind. *How dare he? Why had he? What did he mean?* But what came out was, "What do you mean, you had to see me?"

Instead of answering, he threaded the cord through the metal bracket once more and knotted it, pulling it tight. Then he turned and took a step closer to her. "Could I trouble you for a cup of wine? The journey from our camp is dry and dusty, and longer than it looks."

She did not know what to do. Who was this man, to come barging into her life—into her home—like this? How could he act like this situation was normal when it was anything but? But she suspected that if she wanted answers, she would need to provide the drink to quench his thirst. She went to the table and pulled the cork from the jug. It came off with a hollow pop.

"I took in the cord because I realized you were a liar." She picked up the jug and poured the deep red wine into a cup and held it out.

"How have I lied to you?"

"You told me that your god would bring sure victory. That I would be safe if I helped you."

"And are you not safe?" He took a sip and watched her over the rim of the cup.

"Where is your victory?" She poured herself a cup of the wine as well and set the cork back in the jug. "Is that what you call marching around the city? Is that victory to you?"

"No, marching around the city is not victory. Not yet."

"Then what is it? None have ever heard of an army behaving in such a way. The king is sure his goddess of war has protected the city, and I am not sure I do not believe him."

"Marching around the city is not our victory," Salmon repeated. "It is simply obedience."

"Obedience?"

"To the instructions Yahweh has given to our leader, Joshua. Jericho will be delivered into our hands. The Lord has promised Joshua this, and He will keep His promise. We are marching on His instructions."

"You're telling me that your god, the one you claim is the true and everlasting god, the god who has given you victory over the Amorites and led you into this land—" She broke off to make sure he was still following, and saw him nodding, waiting for her to go on. "He has promised you victory over your enemies and will deliver Jericho into your hands. This god, then, instructed you to march directly to Jericho and…walk silently around the city wall?"

It made no sense. How could he not see how ridiculous this all was?

"For six days," Salmon said, nodding.

"What?"

"He instructed us to walk quietly around the city every day for six days," Salmon said again. "Except for the priests, of course. They must blow the trumpets before the ark of the covenant. So they are not quiet."

She played his words back again in her mind, but they did not make any more sense this time. "I do not understand."

Instead of answering her, he took a seat at the table and gestured for her to sit down beside him. She stood where she was, watching him in the flickering light of the oil lamp.

"Sit, and I will explain everything," he said. "This is why I had to see you. I know that it makes little sense to an outsider, and I wanted to make sure your faith was not wavering."

"It is more than wavering," Rahab said.

"Sit. I will explain all."

And though everything in her told her she should not, that she should kick this man out before he was caught here, that every second in his presence was one step closer to certain death, she found she could not. She wanted to sit next to him. She wanted to hear what she had to say. She wanted to understand more about Yahweh, even if she did not understand why.

Rahab walked over and sat next to him on the bench. She set her cup on the table and said, "Explain, then."

"The ark of the covenant is that box that was carried around the city."

"The gold one. Is that where some secret weapon is stored?"

"That is the presence of the Most High God."

"Your god lives in a box?" At least Ashtart had an altar in the temple.

"He does not live there, exactly. Yahweh is everywhere. He is not constrained by the walls of a temple."

"And yet you put Him in a box."

"The box—the ark of the covenant—reminds us of the promises Yahweh made to our people. Usually it is kept inside the tabernacle, but Yahweh commanded our leader Joshua to have the priests carry it with us into battle."

There were so many things she did not understand.

"The tabernacle?"

"It is a tent. A holy place. The ark sits behind a veil inside the tent. Only the priests are allowed to go near it." He took a sip from his cup. "Someday, when we have taken the land the Lord has promised us, we will build a magnificent temple as a dwelling place for the ark."

So their god would one day have a temple for himself too. Perhaps he was not so different from the gods after all.

"Who are the priests?"

"They are sons of Aaron. Holy and set apart. They offer sacrifices on behalf of our people and teach the law, among other things."

The priests were the religious leaders, then.

"Who is Aaron?"

"The brother of Moses, who led us out of slavery."

She remembered they had been slaves in Egypt until plagues sent by their god had caused Pharoah to release them. The Red Sea parted, soldiers drowned, all that.

133

"You mentioned a covenant Yahweh made with your people. What is that?"

"Yahweh promised our ancestor Abraham that his descendants would be as numerous as the stars in the sky and that His people would call this land their home—all of it, from the wadi in Egypt to the River Euphrates."

Rahab blinked. "You intend to take *all* of it? Every part of that land?" That was basically to the edge of the world. And they believed they would claim it—all of it—for themselves. Rahab felt a new wave of regret wash over her. How had she gotten involved with this misguided group of wanderers? They were delusional, she could see that now. How had she thrown in her lot with them? She should have turned them over to the guards that first night.

She should turn him over to the guards now. Perhaps they would show her mercy, if she confessed. Maybe it was not too late to redeem herself in the eyes of the king.

"We do not take. The Lord gives freely to His chosen people."

Rahab sipped her wine. Outside, she could hear footsteps on the stones of the street, as well as low voices. No doubt people going to make their sacrifices to Ashtart. It was not too late to join them. And yet she did not. She stayed on the bench, seated next to the spy who would no doubt get her killed.

"And is this how you intend to take possession of the whole land?" she asked. "By marching silently—except for the priests—around our city for six days?"

Salmon nodded.

"And you believe that after seeing that, the people of Jericho will simply hand over the city?"

"Oh no." Salmon shook his head. "No, they will not hand it over willingly. Nothing like that."

"So...how will it work, then?"

"I cannot say," he told her.

"Cannot or will not?"

"I do not know. That is the honest truth. But Joshua tells us that on the seventh day, the Lord will deliver Jericho to us. That is when you must gather your family and all who belong to them and make sure you are here, in this room, with the scarlet cord tied to the window."

"Not until the seventh day, then?" Why had he not said so before?

"That is what the Lord has recently revealed to Joshua. Yahweh has promised it. Please, heed the message."

"How can I know it will happen as you say?" Rahab saw that Salmon was closer on the bench than he had been. She could feel the heat from his leg near hers.

"You can know it is true, because Yahweh can be trusted. He is not fickle, like a man. He always keeps His promises to His people."

"Can I trust that you will do the same?"

"You can trust me, Rahab." The way he said it, his voice deep and strong, she almost believed he meant she could trust him for more than this.

She wanted to believe him. She had believed him when he was here last. She had believed in the god who had led the

Israelites to victory. But so much had happened since that night. And after what she had seen today... "I have put myself and my family at great risk to help you."

"And you will be rewarded. We made a covenant with you the night you saved us. We will stand by that, as long as you stand by your part of the covenant."

She must not tell anyone what she knew. She understood. "It is proving difficult to get my family to come to be with me when I cannot tell them why. They would not come today."

"I am sorry, Rahab. Tell them whatever you must to get them here. But you must not tell them about us."

Rahab did not answer. She was busy trying to make sense of all that he had said. She could not, because it did not make sense. His talk of the tabernacle, of priests, of his god who resided in a box—how could he expect her to believe this? How could she trust that simply marching around the city for seven days would allow Yahweh to deliver Jericho into their hands? She had trusted Yahweh, before. Trusted Him enough to put her life at risk and to defy the king's order to make a sacrifice to Ashtart. She wanted to believe again. She wanted to know more about Yahweh, the God who kept His promises. She had never heard of a god like that. Her faith had been shaken by what she had witnessed today, but what if that wasn't the fullness of His plan? What if He truly was going to deliver this land to His people?

"The king believes it was the goddess Ashtart who protected the city today."

"It was not Ashtart. It was not any of the false gods."

"He demands that everyone in town make sacrifices to the war goddess."

"You must not make such a sacrifice to a false god."

"I have not."

"I am glad. Yahweh is the one true God, and He is a jealous God. His people are to make sacrifices to none besides Him."

"I am not one of His people."

"Not yet," Salmon said. "But I have already told you that Yahweh will not forget you. You will be like one of us, when this is all over."

Rahab let those words hang in the air. What if she did not want to be like one of the Israelites? What if she wanted nothing but to live a peaceful life here in Jericho? But she knew that could not happen, not now.

"What you saw today was only the beginning," Salmon said quietly.

And for some reason—through some logic she could never understand—she found she believed him.

She nodded, just a bit. Salmon reached out and put his hand on hers. She should have shrugged it away, but she did not.

"If you only believe, you will see the glory of God."

CHAPTER FIFTEEN

The next morning, Rahab was not surprised when the Israelite army once again marched, two by two, toward Jericho, and slowly began to circle the wall. She could hear neighbors in the building beside her calling down from windows, jeering at the army, and she heard the guards at the corners of the wall moving about, waiting for any unexpected movements. She could see, from her roof, the crowds gathered to worship at the temple of Ashtart and the armed soldiers moving about the city. She watched as, once again, the men with trumpets—the priests—blew out a song, and how the men dressed in the blue robes carried the golden box—the ark of the covenant—carefully around the city walls. They did not attack, nor did they make any noise aside from the trumpets, but they slowly made their way around the city and back to camp.

"Have you seen how weak their army is?" Mostafa asked her in the market that morning. "They do not even try to attack. They simply walk around the wall. What kind of army is this?"

"Is this the mighty army we have been so afraid of?" Shenbar called from the next stall. Things must be different if he was speaking to her—or, if not exactly to her, in her general direction. "They must have seen the might of our army and been too afraid to attack."

"They took one look and marched away," Mostafa added, laughing.

Rahab did not correct them. She knew she could not tell anyone what was really happening, or what *would* happen. She smiled and kept her eyes averted, and she made her purchases quickly.

The very air in the town seemed lighter than it had the day before. People were joking and laughing, relief at having avoided a bloody battle palpable. She heard it in the voices all around her, and she saw it in the posture of Kishar when Rahab went to her sister's home.

"Abu-Waqar believes it is because of how mighty the army is," Kishar said, cradling Ushi to her breast to feed him while they spoke. "That is why the Israelites grew afraid and did not attack. But Gibil tells me King Uz is certain Ashtart has protected us."

"That is why he requires another offering," Hili said, looking up from the wheel where she was spinning wool into fine thread. No doubt working on the cloth for her wedding robes. A wedding that would not happen unless they all listened to her.

"*Another* one?" Rahab had not heard.

"Yes, the announcement was read at the city gates not long after the Israelite army went away in shame this morning," Kishar said. "The messenger came through not long after that. We must find something else to offer."

"Has Ashtart not already had enough of your fine things?"

"She can have all of my fine things if it protects my husband and sons from the battlefield," Kishar said, adjusting

Ushi, who had grasped a chunk of her hair while he fed. "If you had a husband or sons, you would no doubt feel the same."

Rahab bit her lip. Kishar was never cruel. She knew how much it pained Rahab that she had never had sons of her own. But Kishar was wrapped in her own worry now, it seemed, oblivious to the way she'd hurt her sister.

Ashtart was not truly protecting their city. Rahab knew this, but she could not tell her sister—or anyone—what she knew.

"Were you able to find something to offer?" Kishar asked. She did not mean to sound condescending, Rahab knew. But still, Rahab hated the pity in her sister's voice.

Instead of answering, Rahab asked, "What if it's not Ashtart who is keeping them safe?" She adjusted her position on the bench next to Kishar.

"What else could it be?" Hili called. "How else can you explain what happened yesterday, and again today?"

"Hili is right," Kishar said. "Have you ever heard of an army behaving in such a way? If it was not the power of the goddess protecting our city, what could it be?"

"What if the Israelites have a plan? One that we do not expect?" Rahab asked, keeping her voice level. A light breeze shook the palm branches, and the scent of jasmine and orange blossoms filled the small courtyard.

"What kind of plan would it be that involves turning and running the other way after seeing how powerful our city is?" Kishar asked.

Rahab considered how to respond. She realized that she did not need to argue this point. It was not as if Kishar didn't

have enough fine things to offer Ashtart. What mattered was
that she came to Rahab's home on the seventh day.

"I do not know," she said, trying to keep her voice breezy.
"All I know is that on the first day of the week, you must come
to my home," Rahab said. "Before the sun is up, you must be
there."

"Do not start this again." Kishar let out a sigh. "I had hoped
we could move past that strange request. It did not turn out to
be necessary, did it?"

"It did not, yet," Rahab agreed. "But it will. Please, come on
the seventh day."

"You visited Nuesh and Sagma to give them the same message," Kishar said. "Mama and Father too. Mama thinks the
stress is starting to affect you."

"The stress is not getting to me." Rahab did not intend for
the firm edge in her voice. "I cannot say more than this. But
please, on the seventh day, come."

"The Israelites will be long gone by the seventh day," Hili
said. "There is no way we will need to worry about them by
then."

Rahab did not answer. Ushi struggled to get up, and Kishar
pulled him away from her and let her robe fall closed. She set
the child on her knee.

"I just hope Abu-Waqar and the boys are allowed to come
home tonight," Kishar said. "They have not slept at home in
two nights."

Kishar was changing the subject, Rahab understood. She
reluctantly let her, knowing that continuing to argue with her

141

sister would only result in pushing Kishar further away. She hoped she would be able to convince her before the time came. For now, she said, "Surely they will be allowed to come home soon, if the offerings to Ashtart are appeasing the goddess of war."

The conversation continued, but they never managed to get past the awkwardness. Kishar did not believe Rahab. Rahab's own faith had wavered, and she had met the Israelite men and learned about their god. Of course Kishar did not understand. Who had ever heard of a god who showed his might not with swords and arrows but with music and silent obedience? Rahab returned home, determined to try again with her sister the next day, after the Israelites marched around the city gate once more.

When Rahab returned home, however, she found guards flanking her door, surrounding Penzer, the tax collector. She saw that Hili's betrothed, Gal, was among the half-dozen guards at her door this time. Rahab felt a stab of fear. What did he want now? Her debts had been paid in full. He could not seriously still think he could collect from her now.

"Hello, Penzer," Rahab said, moving toward her door. The guards did not clear out to make way for her. "It is nice of you to call on me for a change. Normally I must make the trip to your office myself."

"This is no time for joking, Rahab. I am here on serious business from the king."

"So I see." She gestured at the half-dozen guards flanking him. "You have brought protection."

"They are not here to protect me," Penzer said.

"Have you come to arrest me, then? For what cause?"

"I am here to make sure you have heard the message that every citizen of Jericho is required to make offerings to Ashtart, the goddess of war, whose protection has kept this city safe."

"I have heard," Rahab said. She decided it was best not to say more.

"And yet you have not made one offering, let alone the three that King Uz has required."

She blinked. She had not known the leaders would be tracking who made sacrifices to Ashtart and who did not. She felt like a fool now. She should have guessed. But would it have changed anything, had she known? She knew it would not have.

"I was not aware that you were in charge of monitoring the citizens' sacrifices to the gods, in addition to their taxes," Rahab said. "That is a promotion for you, is it not?"

"I am in charge of making sure all that is due our king and those who support him is paid," Penzer said, raising his voice a bit. "And while you may no longer owe back taxes, you owe sacrifices."

"Is it not unusual for the man in charge of taxes to also be in charge of holy sacrifices to deities?" Rahab could not stop herself from asking. "Would that not be the place of one of the temple guards?" Was the king keeping the goods sacrificed to the goddess for himself? But how could that be, if they were intended for the goddess?

"It is unusual for a woman, particularly a woman of your station, to insult a messenger of the king and ignore his majesty's orders," Penzer said, his eyebrows arched, his voice imperious.

"I assure you, I did not mean to insult a man of such stature," Rahab said, though she had meant precisely that. "I simply was pleased that the king has finally recognized your talent and expanded your duties." The flattery was too obvious. It sounded insincere even to her own ears, but the way Penzer stood up a bit straighter on hearing the words made her realize they had had their intended effect.

"The king requires for me to take what is owed," Penzer said. "You are required to make your sacrifice to Ashtart by nightfall."

Rahab could not make a sacrifice to the goddess she knew to be false. But she did not know what to say to get out of it.

"I will," she said, nodding. She needed time to think. She would find another way to get out of making the sacrifice. She would—

"If you cannot afford anything to sacrifice," Penzer said, his eyes moving down from her face to her body, "there is another way to appease Ashtart."

Rahab felt bile rise up in her throat. Not again. She would rather go to prison than to give her body to this man again. She saw that the guards standing by had all averted their eyes, pretending they could not hear what was being said.

"Surely the goddess of war could not be appeased by such things," Rahab said.

Penzer took a step closer to her. "Ashtart is not just the goddess of war," he said. "She is also the goddess of...other things."

Rahab stepped back. She knew that Ashtart was worshiped as the goddess of relations between a man and a woman, in addition to the goddess of war. It was no small wonder she was the favorite goddess of so many men, including King Uz. Any man with that many wives and concubines could not help but worship at her altar.

"I do not see how that will help the king's efforts to fight back the Israelites," Rahab said.

"The Israelites are running scared. That is how powerful Ashtart is. The weaklings do not dare to attack our city because of her power," Penzer said. He reached out and put his hand on her arm. "And this act would bring her joy."

It would bring him joy—him and him alone. She pulled her arm away.

"I will bring my sacrifice before daybreak," she said, knowing she would not. She turned and went back inside and closed the door behind her, and, after a few moments, Penzer and the guards reluctantly marched away.

Rahab went inside and started cooking for Garza and Gishimar. Gishimar did not seem to mind being away from his family a few extra days, but Garza had begun to complain about being locked inside a besieged city and the astronomical cost of his bill. Rahab ignored him and waited for nightfall. Waited to see if Salmon would come back.

CHAPTER SIXTEEN

Salmon called her name shortly after Garza and Gishimar had gone up to bed. Rahab had taken her time with the dishes tonight, hoping he might come back. Salmon had not told her he would, and she knew it was foolishness, that if he was seen, it would mean death for them both, but somehow, she still hoped he would come back to see her tonight. It was silly. She was not some girl who could flirt with the young men in the marketplace—she was a grown woman whose very life was in danger—and yet she still felt a fluttering excitement in her belly when she thought that he might come. And here he was, climbing up the rope and over the windowsill and into her home.

"You came back," she said, feeling her cheeks flush. "It was very silly for you to come back."

"I had to see you," he said, brushing off his robes once more. "I needed to make sure you were not going to do something foolish like pulling in the scarlet cord again."

"I have not," Rahab said. Neither one of them spoke for a moment, and they stood a short distance apart, gazing at one another. "It is not safe for you to be here."

"And yet you do not insist I leave." He smiled at her, looking deep into her eyes, and all the arguments she had for why he needed to leave went right out of her head. "May I have some wine? I am thirsty from my walk."

She nodded and walked to the kitchen and pulled the jug from its shelf. "How is it that you are not seen as you walk from your camp? The guards are watching from every corner of the city wall."

"I told you last night, the Lord has closed their eyes."

"That does not make any sense." She pulled the cork out and poured wine into two cups.

"And yet here I am."

"Perhaps they have seen you and will be coming to arrest us both now." She handed out one cup to him, and he took it and gulped down the drink. "Perhaps your recklessness will cost us both our lives."

"Perhaps it will," he said. "But despite that, you let me in." He met her eye once again. He held her gaze, and though neither said a word, he somehow told her everything she wanted to know. That he felt the same excitement seeing her that she felt at seeing him. That he had come here not just to make sure she did not pull in the cord. That he had risked his life and hers because he had wanted to see her again.

"It is foolishness." Never mind the guards on the walls. If he was discovered here by anyone, any shred of respectability Rahab had managed to gain would be torn away instantly. Ladies did not entertain men alone at night. People would assume the worst. She would be in even worse shape than she currently was.

Then again, she did not have far to fall. What harm could it really do to be seen with a handsome man, when everyone already thought her a harlot? She could hardly stain her reputation more than it already was.

Instead of answering, he held out his cup, and she filled it again before following him to the table, just as she had known she would. He sat with his body angled toward her.

"What is the news in Jericho?" Salmon asked. "How did people react when they saw our army march around the city once again?"

"They did not understand it. They think your army is weak, that you are afraid to attack. They are quite giddy, in fact, believing that the goddess of war has protected us."

He nodded, curling his fingers around the cup. "This goddess has no power. Only Yahweh has true power."

"King Uz does not know that. He is demanding that everyone in Jericho make sacrifices to the goddess Ashtart."

"And have you?"

"I have not." She heard a noise upstairs, one of the guests moving around. But then all was quiet once again. "I believe that Yahweh is more powerful."

"I am glad of it," Salmon said. "Yahweh had commanded His people not to bow down before any idols. We must sacrifice only to Yahweh."

"I am not one of your people," Rahab said.

"Not yet." He met her eye over the top of her cup. "You are not bound by our covenant, but you know that this goddess of war is nothing but a false idol."

"The king's men came with guards tonight. They threatened to arrest me if I did not comply." She did not tell him the other option Penzer had offered. "I am to make a sacrifice before daybreak."

"That is terrible. We cannot let that happen."

"I have been trying to come up with an idea for how to appease the king without offering a sacrifice, but I have no good ideas."

Both were quiet for a moment. Salmon was gazing past her, at the wall behind. Then, finally, he said, "People see what they want to see."

"What?" Rahab did not understand what he was trying to tell her.

"If they want to see you making a sacrifice, let them see you making a sacrifice."

Rahab had not heard him correctly, she was sure of it. "You have just told me I must not make a sacrifice to a piece of ivory."

"Do not actually make a sacrifice," Salmon said. "But perhaps if you go there, that will be enough. Where are the sacrifices to be made?"

"The temple of the gods. It is near the palace."

"If you go there, you will be seen, and—"

"What if I am not seen?"

"No man could fail to notice a woman as beautiful as you," Salmon said. Rahab's breath caught, but he continued on. "They will remember you were there. Perhaps they will not notice if you do not make an actual sacrifice. They will know you were there and see what they want to see."

Rahab did not see how that could work. But she had no better ideas.

"I guess it may be worth a try. I must find some way to appease the king."

"Perhaps appeasing the king is not as important as you think it is."

Rahab narrowed her eyes. "That is easy for you to say. You will climb out through the window and go back to your people tonight. You will not have to face the wrath and scorn of the king and all the people."

"You may have to face their wrath and scorn for a few days. But you will soon see redemption."

She shook her head. "You speak of the destruction of this city and its people like it is some glorious thing. It is not glorious. It is terrible."

Salmon took in a deep breath and nodded. He scratched at his beard. "You are right, of course. The taking of a city is not a thing to glorify. The loss of life is a tragedy."

"In that case, tell me again why you must take this city?" Rahab asked. "Cannot you simply talk with the king and try to work out an arrangement to share the land? Is it really necessary to *conquer* the land?"

"It is because the Lord has commanded it," Salmon said. "Because He has given this land to our people. His people."

"And what makes your people so special to Yahweh?"

"It is because of the covenant He made with Abraham."

"You mentioned Abraham before. The man whose descendants would be as numerous as the stars of the sky."

"That is right."

"What is his story?"

And then Salmon told her an incredible story, too fantastic to be believed. He spoke of a promise Yahweh had made to Abram, a man who was childless, to make his descendants as numerous as the stars in the sky, and then of the two children born to him, Isaac and Ishmael. He told her of Abram offering his son on an altar to the Lord, and how the Lord saved Isaac only at the last moment. He spoke of a son sold into slavery by his jealous brothers, and how Yahweh used him to save his people from a famine. He told her how his ancestors had gone to Egypt, where they were enslaved, and how Yahweh sent ten plagues on the Egyptians until Pharaoh agreed to free them, and how they walked across the Red Sea as if on dry land. He told her about a promise to give the Israelites a homeland, and a burning bush, and a mountain, and stone tablets on which were inscribed the Law. He also told her how his people's disobedience had led to forty years of wandering in the desert, and how none of his parents' generation was left to cross the Jordan River into the Promised Land. And he told her how the Lord had led them to the land that was their inheritance, and how their enemies had fallen before them.

"It sounds impossible," Rahab said when he had finished. Their cups were long empty, and the sounds of the city had quieted around them. She did not know how late it was, but they had been talking for many hours.

"Which part?" In the time they had been talking, Salmon had somehow moved closer to her without either of them

151

noticing, and his knee was pressed against hers. She hated herself for wanting him closer.

"All of it. Every part of the story sounds impossible."

"And yet it is true." He smiled. "Nothing is impossible for the Lord."

And once again, though she could not say why, Rahab believed him.

"Stay strong, Rahab," he told her. "The Lord's protection will be upon you."

He held her hand for a moment before he left, leaving her more confused than ever.

On the third day, the Israelites marched around the city once again, and the people of Jericho called down insults and threw rotten food at the Israelites, laughing and jeering, and they let out a cheer as the army began its long march back to its camp. Those in the town were growing cocky, believing their own might and power had sent the Israelite army away. They were such fools, Rahab thought. They had no clue what was coming. Salmon glanced up at her window as he marched past, and she felt a thrill, knowing he was thinking of her.

Once again, an announcement was sent through the town that the king demanded another sacrifice to Ashtart. "King Uz, in his great wisdom, requires all citizens of Jericho to make a sacrifice to Ashtart, the goddess of war, whose great power has protected this city this day."

This time, Rahab did not ignore the message. This day, after she had fetched the water and cleaned up after the morning meal, she tied her bag to her waist and put on her traveling cloak and headed out. She went first to the city gates and spoke to Munzur, who told her that the guards at the gate were growing cocky.

"They believe they have scared the Israelites away," Munzur said. He took the crusts of bread from her greedily. "They honestly believe their spears and shields have frightened them."

"You do not think so?" Rahab asked.

"If this is the same army that leveled the kingdoms of Sihon and Og, then no. This is a trick. They have something planned and are biding their time," Munzur said through a mouthful of bread.

Rahab walked away, wondering how the fool at the city gates was the only one who could see the truth, while everyone else in the town seemed so certain that the Israelites were too afraid to attack. She went first to the marketplace, where the vegetables were mostly limp and starting to mold and the meat beginning to turn rancid. With the gates closed, no one could go in or out, and fresh food was growing scarce. Rahab bought lentils and some dried lamb and listened as the vendors joked with the women in the market about how long it would be before the Israelites gave up and returned to whatever backwater they had come from.

When Rahab had bought what scarce supplies she could, she joined the crowd making its way up the hill toward the temple of Ashtart, which was adjacent to the palace. A lush garden separated the king's home from the home of the gods. Rahab had played in that garden when she was a girl, laughing and running with the other children of Uz's father's high-ranking officials. But now, the fence that led to the garden was guarded by men in armor and swords. The stone edifice of the temple reached high into the sky, the golden stone gleaming in the sunshine. Rahab stood with the crowd that gathered in the courtyard, pressed up closely one against another and jostling its way slowly inside. Rahab saw her sister Ri on the far side of the crowd, but if Ri saw her, she did not acknowledge her. Slowly, eventually, she and those around her made their way toward the doors of the temple, which had been thrown wide open, guards on either side. Rahab carried her shopping basket in her arms, the food covered with a cloth, and she hoped those around her would assume the contents were her offering to the goddess.

Inside, the temple had high ceilings and walls decorated with rich blue and gold paint. An altar stood on a raised dais at the far end of the room. Rahab was pulled, along with the others, toward the altar, where citizens were meant to leave their offerings. Rahab knew the goddess herself—or, at least, the icon they worshiped as the goddess—was in an interior room, protected from the sight of the crowds. Rahab watched as each person in the crowd placed an object of great worth on the temple altar—she saw golden earrings and bangles, metal tools, fine cloth, and simple coins. Each person brought what they could, and as quickly as they laid their offerings down, guards removed the riches, placing the items in large bags at their feet. Rahab recognized two of the guards who had been at her door last night, demanding she appear in the temple with her offering. Well, she was here now, and she made sure she caught the eye of one of the guards as she was moved, along with the crowd, toward the altar.

Rahab wondered what would be done with the items once they were laid at the feet of the goddess. She supposed they probably became the property of the king. Whether or not Ashtart was truly protecting the city, the King Uz was doing well in this exchange. It was no wonder Penzer, manager of the king's accounts, was keeping such a close eye on the offerings.

Rahab let herself be moved toward the altar, but before she reached it, she turned and pressed her way to the side, making her exit before she had to appear at the altar empty-handed. She let herself be drawn, along with the crowd, toward the side door, where citizens were streaming out of the temple and out the side gate that led back to the street. Rahab hoped her appearance here had been enough, and that the guards would report to Penzer that Rahab had appeared to make her offering.

And she hoped Yahweh would know that she had not actually done so. Yahweh wanted His people to worship no other gods before Him, Salmon had told her. Well, she was throwing in her lot with Yahweh and His people, come what may. It was too late to change her mind now.

CHAPTER SEVENTEEN

Rahab was not surprised when Salmon appeared outside her window that night. She had been waiting, cleaning the main room until it was spotless, telling herself it did not matter if he came or not. She would not be disappointed if he could not come this night. It would be better, in fact—he would not put both their lives in danger if he stayed away. But when she heard him call to her from outside the window, she quickly tossed down the rope she'd left tied next to the scarlet cord, and he climbed inside the window, a goofy smile on his face.

"You were waiting for me," he said as he brushed off his robes.

"I was not. I was cleaning," Rahab said, pointing at the rag she had been using to wipe the dishes clean.

"It is a strange hour to clean," Salmon said, stepping toward her. "Most women do that chore during the daylight."

"I am very busy, running an inn by myself," Rahab said. "I must do chores at all hours."

"You were waiting for me." He stepped forward again, grinned. "I am glad. I could not wait to see you again either. I have thought of nothing but you since I left here last night."

Rahab sputtered, trying to think of a reply that did not sound foolish, but Salmon did not wait for a response. He strode past her, walked into the kitchen area, and pulled the jug of wine down off the shelf himself.

"Let me do that," Rahab said, but Salmon was already pouring wine from the jug into the cups.

"I am parched," he said. "And I want nothing more than to sit beside the most beautiful woman I have ever seen."

"You flatter me." But Rahab took the cup and followed him to the now-familiar spot on the bench.

"I speak the truth." He lowered himself down onto the bench, and when she sat beside him, he shifted to move his body closer. "What happened inside the city today?"

Rahab had the fleeting thought that he always asked about what was happening inside the city. Was he here not just to see her, as he claimed? Or did he risk his life and hers to get a report from inside the city? He was a spy, after all. Was she nothing but a source for him?

But the way he was looking at her now—as if he couldn't take his eyes off of her, as if he never wanted to look away—made her believe it was more than that. Mashda had gazed at her as a child gazed at a new toy, while Pezner and the others had always betrayed nothing but greedy desire. The only person who had ever looked at her this way, with such tenderness, was Minesh, who she had loved as a child. Though it had been many years, she knew the look, deep in her soul.

"Much the same," Rahab said. "The king grows cocky. He still believes his might and the goddess Ashtart are what are keeping your army from attacking."

"He will be very disappointed when he learns the truth."

"I think it's safe to say he will be more than disappointed." King Uz would be… Well, he would be dead. His city destroyed, and all within it. It was unthinkable. The idea of everything she'd ever known, all the people she saw each day, simply gone—it was too horrible. She decided to press him again. "Is there truly no other way? No path but total destruction?"

"Not unless your king gives his land willingly."

"That is not likely to happen." The king was no doubt too busy counting the spoils from his recent decrees to consider that he might do something differently.

"In that case, we have no choice but to take it. This is the land Yahweh has given us."

But the land was already inhabited by other people. Good people. People with families and lives they had built for themselves. It was not their fault they happened to reside in the land Yahweh wanted to give the Israelites.

"Here is what I do not understand. If He really is as powerful as you say—"

"He is."

Rahab nodded. "I do not doubt it. But if He truly is the most powerful of all gods, why can He not find another way? One that does not mean so many innocent people have to die?"

Mostafa. Haran. Munzur. Hili's betrothed Gal. Would they truly all be dead just a few days from now?

"Do you suppose the people would simply choose to let us live beside them? To give up their gods and worship Yahweh alone? To give over the land that is our inheritance?"

"I do not know. But might He not try? If He is the one true God, surely He would have the power to make it so?"

Salmon did not answer for a moment. He looked at her. He almost seemed as though he was looking through her.

"It is not for us to understand the ways of the Lord," he finally said. "I do not understand why He is having us do this. What I do know is this: The Lord God is good. He is just. And He will use all things for His plans. As hard as it is to trust and believe His words, that is what He requires of us."

Rahab bit back the words that threatened to come out, but Salmon touched her arm.

"What is it? I can see that you want to say something."

Rahab did not dare. She could not say what she thought.

"You will not scare me away," Salmon said, "And the Lord can handle your questions."

Rahab was not sure this was true. But she decided she did not have much to lose at this stage. "When you speak of Him that way, He does not seem like a wise and powerful God. He seems more like a father who plays favorites, giving toys to the ones He likes best and taking them from the rest."

She was not sure how she had been expecting Salmon to respond, but she had not expected the laughter that filled the room. He had a deep, warm laugh, and she could not help but feel lighter at the sound.

"Yes, I suppose He does, in some ways," Salmon said. "But He created the world and all that is in it. It is His to give and take, as He pleases."

She supposed one could see it that way.

"I cannot tell you the mind of God," Salmon said. "I cannot explain why He does what He does. I can only tell you what I have seen: I have seen Him provide for His people, sending food from the heavens, every day of my life. I have seen Him dry up the waters of the Jordan River and allow every member of our group to walk across the riverbed on dry land. I have seen mighty kingdoms fall before the power of His hand, just as He promised. I do not understand everything the Lord thinks or does, but I know that He will do exactly as He says, and I know I can trust in Him."

It did not answer Rahab's questions. She still had so many confused thoughts and beliefs. She had so many things she wanted to ask and questions she wanted answered. But more than that, she wanted what Salmon had. She wanted the kind of deep faith that allowed Salmon to know that the Lord God was working on his behalf, even when he did not understand how. To know, because of what he'd seen with his own eyes, that Yahweh would do exactly what He promised He would do. To trust that she did not have to worry about how or why, only to believe and obey.

Salmon's hand was still on her arm, and slowly, he began to trace his fingers gently down the skin of her arms to her wrist. Her breath caught, as, softly, gently, his fingers found her hand. He should not be touching her like this. She should not be letting him touch her like this. This was wildly dangerous. If anyone saw them like this—

And yet she could not bring herself to pull her hand away. His fingertips were rough, but his touch was gentle as he let his fingers explore her palm, tracing the lines, exploring every inch of her fingers with his. All of the questions she had about Yahweh had somehow gone out of her head.

The way he was looking at her, as if he never wanted to pull his hand away, as if he wanted to know more of her, made her sure he was feeling the same way she was. She tried to make herself answer but found she could not come up with the words. Before she knew what was happening, he began to lean in toward her, and she knew she did not want him to stop.

A knock on the door caused them both to jump back.

"Rahab!"

It couldn't be. It sounded like—

"Rahab, open up."

Kishar. She was rattling the door handle now.

"It is my sister." Rahab's eyes flew to the door, and she was horrified to see that she had neglected to set the bar into the hooks. Kishar could simply open the door.

But she would never. Kishar had never entered Rahab's home, not since—

Rahab jumped up and rushed toward the door, but she was too late. Kishar had pushed open the door and was walking into the room.

"Rahab, is it true? Abu-Waqar tells me you have not yet made even one sacrifice to Ashtart. I came here to beg you. They are talking of arresting—"

Kishar froze.

"Oh." Kishar's mouth dropped open, seeing Salmon, taking in the two cups, the dimly lit room. "Who—"

161

"Hello, Kishar," Rahab said. "I did not expect you."

"No, I see that." Kishar's eyes were wide. "I did not think you would be with a...a customer."

"He is not a customer!" Rahab said quickly, and then instantly regretted it. Better to have her sister think she was a harlot indeed than have her learn the truth. "He is—" Her mind was empty, dulled by the competing emotions rushing through her.

But Salmon had already pushed himself up and was striding toward the door.

"Salmon," he said, bowing his head. "It is a pleasure to meet you."

What was he doing? He could not truly be telling her his name.

"He is—" Rahab broke off. What would her sister believe? "A friend."

"A friend." Kishar looked from Rahab to Salmon and back again. "It is an odd time for entertaining."

"It is my fault," Salmon said smoothly. "I came uninvited, to tell you the truth."

"And where did you come from, Salmon?" Kishar asked. Rahab saw that her sister had noticed that he did not wear the rope belt that was so common in Jericho, that his features were finer and his skin darker than most in this region.

"I am from nowhere in particular, at the moment," Salmon said. "Though I am very much enjoying my time in Jericho."

"You are...a guest at my sister's inn?" Kishar asked tentatively. Rahab could see she wanted to believe it, though she had doubts.

"Yes," Rahab said, just as Salmon answered, "No."

"Which is it, then?"

"No," Salmon said. "As I said, I came in uninvited. The truth is, I am an Israelite."

Rahab was not sure who gasped louder, herself or her sister. Kishar was already backing up, toward the door. What was he doing, speaking the truth this way? He was going to get himself killed. He was going to ruin everything.

"He is not," Rahab said quickly, but again, Salmon disagreed with her.

"I am part of the Israelite army," Salmon said. "Your sister has been kind to me."

"It is true, then," Kishar hissed. "They were here. You hid them that night."

"I—"

"Your sister has shown me great kindness."

"And the cloth. This is where you got it? As payment for protecting our enemies?"

"It is not like that," Rahab said, trying to make her sister understand.

"Did you even need that money to pay down your debts? Or was that a lie too? Did that money go straight into the pockets of our enemies?"

"Please, just listen. It is not like that."

"It is like that, I'm afraid," Salmon said. Rahab turned to him, her mouth open. What did he think he was doing?

"I should have known. I should never have believed you." Kishar's voice was raised, but Rahab dared not shush her.

"I asked Rahab not to say a word," Salmon said. He stepped up next to Rahab and placed a hand on her back. "I gave her my word that she and all who are here in the home with the scarlet cord will not perish when the city falls. She swore an oath not to tell anyone. But she could not convince you to come here, so I am telling you myself. When Jericho falls, you must be here, in your sister's home. Tell your family to be here, all of them."

"Salmon." Rahab turned to him. "They will kill you."

"Perhaps they will," Salmon said. "It does not matter if I live or die. Only that Yahweh's promise be fulfilled. Jericho will fall to the Israelites, with or without me. My only thought now is making sure you and your family are safe when it does."

"I will tell," Kishar said. "I will go home and tell Abu-Waqar right now. I will let him know that you are a traitor, that you are helping our enemies. I will tell him you are a harlot indeed."

"Kishar, please listen," Rahab said. She hated how much the words stung. "Salmon is good. He is kind. He is going to keep us safe."

"Keep us safe from his incompetent army, you mean?" Kishar spat.

"Just listen—"

"No, Rahab, listen to me. I have always defended you. I have always taken your side. Even when you have disgraced our family name, I have stood by you. But this time, you have gone too far. This time, you have put all of our lives in danger—"

"That's just it," Rahab said. "Our lives will be lost if you do not listen to me. This is what I have been trying to tell you. This is why you need to come to be here with me, to be here on the seventh day."

"Why? So we can be arrested for treason? So we can be executed as enemies of the very king my husband is pledged to serve?"

"To be saved," Salmon said. "Your sister has asked you to be here because she is a good woman, of strong character, and trustworthy. She has told you to come because she loves you, you and all your family, and she wants you to be saved."

Something about the strong, calm tone of Salmon's voice seemed to quiet Kishar. When she spoke again, her voice was not as shrill.

"Saved from what?" she asked. "From the army that marches in circles but dares not take on our army?"

"Saved from what is coming. From what will happen to Jericho when the Lord makes His power known."

"And what is that?" Kishar asked. She had lowered her voice, but her tone was still defiant. "What will happen? Do you honestly believe that your trumpets and your golden box will defeat the strongest army in all of the land of Canaan?"

"Yours is not the strongest army in Canaan," Salmon said. "Not by far. The Amorites were stronger, and we did not lose a single man when we took the kingdoms of Sihon and Og. But it is not the might of our army that allowed for our victory. It was the power of our God."

"Can you really believe this Yahweh you worship is stronger than Ashtart, the goddess of war?"

"I know He is. So too did the Amorites, just before the end."

Kishar reached out a hand to the wall to steady herself.

"They too offered sacrifices to Ashtart," Salmon continued. "The goddess did not save them, and she will not save you either. Only Yahweh can do that."

"It is not true." Kishar's voice was quieter.

"Come, be with your sister when she calls you. Bring your children."

Kishar turned to Rahab. "Do you believe this too? Do you believe in the power of this Yahweh?"

"I do," Rahab said. "I have seen His power myself. I have seen how He protected the spies. How He shuts the eyes of the guards to keep His servant safe. I know it to be true."

"You are one of them," she said. "You have abandoned your family and your people, and you have joined the enemy."

"I have not," Rahab said.

But Kishar wasn't listening.

"It is no wonder you have not made your sacrifice to the goddess," she said. "Because you do not even want our army to win."

"That is not true. I would give anything for things to go back the way they were. But this is something that cannot be stopped."

"I do not know who you are anymore," Kishar said. She was looking directly at Rahab, speaking only to her sister. "I do not understand what happened to you."

"I do not mind if you hate me. I do not care if you never speak to me again when all this is over. Only come, you and your family. Bring our mother and father, our brothers and sisters. In four days, come here, and you will be safe."

Kishar looked from Rahab to Salmon, his hand on Rahab's back, and then back at her sister. And then she turned and walked out, not saying another word.

As soon as the door closed behind her, Rahab felt the strength go out of her legs. Dark spots appeared in her eyes, and her knees started to buckle, but Salmon leaned in to her held her up so she did not fall. His strength made her feel stronger.

"You should go," she finally said, once her vision had cleared again. "Quickly. Go before my sister sends the king's guards to arrest us both. They will be here in minutes, no doubt."

Kishar would tell Abu-Waqar, and he would sound the alarm. The guards would not wait for daybreak. They would come quickly, hoping to catch Salmon before he escaped.

"I will not leave you," he said. "If they come, they come for both of us."

"It will be worse if we are caught together," Rahab said. "Please, go now, before the guards show up."

Ignoring her words, he led her back to the table and sat her down. "Your lives for our lives. That is what we said that night. I have put you in danger coming here, and I will be right here beside you if they come for you."

She wanted to argue more with him, but found she could not. Instead, she sat slumped against him, waiting for the knock that would announce that the guards had come for them.

Waiting for the knock that never came.

They sat up all night, sitting together, her body resting against his, just sitting. Waiting. They sat there until daylight began to brighten the horizon, and Salmon knew he must go.

"She did not tell," he said, as he slung his leg over the sash of the window and began to climb down the rope. "Your sister has protected you."

Rahab realized he was right, for now at least. "She has not told anyone yet," she said. "But I do not know how long she will keep quiet."

"Let us hope it will be long enough." Then he leaned back inside, kissed Rahab on the cheek, and disappeared out the window.

CHAPTER EIGHTEEN

Rahab lay down on her mat, but she did not sleep, and she got up again when she heard Garza moving around in his room. She did not want to do anything but lie there, hoping against hope that her sister would not tell what she had seen, but Rahab could not. She still had to draw water, she still had to feed her guests. She must go through the rhythms of the day as if all were normal, as if everything hadn't changed dramatically—again—last night.

She pulled her robe around herself and made her way downstairs. They sun was higher than when she normally rose, and the air was already hot. Out the window, she could see that the Israelite army was already beginning its long march across the valley for what would be its fourth loop around the city walls. She did not wait and watch. She made the meal for Garza and Gishimar, and she talked to them while they ate, just like she did on any other day.

"How many times do you suppose they are going to do that?" Garza asked, nodding his head toward the window. The sound of thousands of footsteps and metal clanking against metal filled the air.

"I do not know," Rahab said. Her voice sounded weak to her, but Garza did not seem to notice.

"Perhaps they will give up today," Gishimar continued, raising his voice to be heard over the trumpets that were passing by this stretch of the wall. "And then I can go home to Jerusalem."

"Perhaps they will," Rahab said. She knew they would not. "It will be good for you to see your family again." She knew Gishimar had two small daughters back in Jerusalem. He spoke of them often.

"It will," Garza agreed. "You have been an admirable hostess. But it has been quite difficult to be stuck in a city that is under siege."

"It has indeed," Rahab said. And then, after a moment, she added, "You must stay here."

"What?" He looked up at her.

"If—" How could she say this? "If anything happens to me. If I am not here. Please, continue to stay here. You will be safe."

"What are you saying?" Garza narrowed his eyes. "Where would you go? The city is closed up. No one can go in or out."

"I am not planning to go anywhere," Rahab said. "But— just in case. You will be safe here."

"I do not know that any of us are safe," Garza said, returning to his flatbread.

Once she had cleaned up the meal and Garza and Gishimar had gone off to do—well, whatever it was they did these days— Rahab took her bag and headed out to the market. But she had not gone very far when she was met by a phalanx of the king's guards.

"Rahab," the one in front called, "you are under arrest, by order of the king." Behind him were half a dozen guards.

They were just going to do it right here, then, out in the
street. The people streamed past on both sides, trying to get
past the group of guards that was blocking much of the pas-
sageway. They were not going to take her somewhere private.
They probably preferred to do it this way, out in the open. The
better to warn the others in the city what happened when you
defied the king.

"For what charge?" At least Kishar had waited until Salmon
was gone to report her. At least he would not be taken as well.

"For failure to worship the goddess Ashtart and give your
sacrifices to her," the lead guard said.

For failing to worship Ashtart? Not for Salmon, then?

For a moment, she felt a sense of relief wash over her. They
weren't arresting her for harboring a spy. They didn't know
about Salmon.

But that sense of relief was fleeting. She was still under
arrest. The outcome would not be different for this arrest. She
was guilty in both cases.

The guard had already taken her hands and was tying
them behind her back with a thick rope. He pulled the rope
tight, and it burned against her skin, but she did not cry out.

"Come." He pulled on the rope, and she was forced to walk.
He held on to the rope as he began to lead her through the
streets.

"Harlot," she heard whispered as she walked. The guards
on either side of her did not look at her, but they too joined in
the name-calling as they walked. "Traitor," the one on her left
said several times as they walked. He tried to trip her with his

171

spear. One of them spit at her, though she did not see which. "Harlot."

Around her, people scurried by, many carrying offerings to once again lay at the altar of the goddess Ashtart.

Rahab kept her eyes cast down so she could not see the looks of scorn on the faces of those who passed by. She could see that she was not being led down into the prison, though. Not yet, anyway. Instead, she was being taken past the temple and into a door at the back of the palace. It was the door used by the men and women who worked at the palace. Rahab had been through it many times when she was a child. Once inside, they were met by more guards. The guards took her down a long hallway, dim and stinking of onions and garbage, and then up a flight of stone stairs. The metal of the guards' armor clinked as they led her down another hallway, this one wider, with high ceilings and polished marble floors. Rahab had never been to this part of the palace, but she was pretty sure she knew where she was being led.

They turned a corner, and then she was faced with tall wooden doors, carved with scenes from Jericho's glorious past. She saw carved into the wood the meeting between the moon god Yarikh and the first king of Jericho, King Zasmin, when Yarikh promised to protect and guide the city for all of its days. Rahab had heard the story many times through the years, but now she knew it was nothing but a story. She also saw scenes of previous kings vanquishing enemies in battle and, on the bottom panel, of King Uz battling his brother Ultultar for the throne and rising victorious. That carving must have been added the most recently.

Rahab did not know how long she stood with the guards outside the doors of the throne room, but her back began to ache and her feet grew sore. The high windows were open, but the air in the space was still, and the many bodies pressed together made it feel hot and stuffy. She was thirsty and hungry and so weary she felt like she might fall over on her feet, but she was kept awake by the guards who stood around her, hissing at her under their breath.

"Harlot."

"Traitor."

Finally, when Rahab was growing fearful she might collapse on her feet, the doors opened, and she was led inside. Rahab had never been inside the throne room before. She had never seen a room so opulent. The ceilings soared far above the ground and the stone of the floor was polished to a high sheen. A long aisle ran to the front of the room, and along both sides of the aisle guards stood at attention, facing each other as Rahab was led inside. At the far end, beneath a window of splendid colors, there was a raised platform, and on it sat a golden throne, carved with intricate designs and larger than any chair Rahab had ever seen. The floor beneath it was inlaid with gold in a pattern that she recognized as the symbol of the king's family.

The guards gave her a shove, and Rahab realized she was being told to walk toward the king. In front of her, King Uz sat on the throne, wrapped in a robe of the deepest indigo. A golden crown sat on his head, and he stared down at her with a look of disdain and disgust as she marched forward. Her footsteps sounded on the floor, echoing in the cavernous room. He looked powerful, she thought, and important. But he also looked young, with round cheeks and an awkward carriage he had not yet grown into. He looked, Rahab thought, like a boy playing king.

"What charge is leveled against this woman?" The king's face may have been young, but his voice was deep.

"She has failed to offer the required sacrifices to the goddess Ashtart, Your Majesty." It was Penzer who spoke. Rahab had not noticed him standing to the side, near the front of the room. There were other men in fine robes there. She scanned quickly, hoping to see her brother's face, but Gibil was not among them. "She has only appeared at the temple one time, and she did not make a sacrifice that day."

So the guards had noticed, then. The plan had not worked. But they did not say anything about Salmon, about helping the spies or being caught consorting with one of them. Had Kishar not yet raised the alarm? Or were they simply biding their time?

The king turned back to Rahab. "Is it true? Have you neglected to make your offerings to the goddess?"

"It is true, your grace." It came out much more softly than she had intended, swallowed by the vastness of the room.

"What was that? Speak up." The king did not have any trouble being heard. His voice boomed, echoing off the polished floor.

"It is true," Rahab said more loudly this time.

"And why have you ignored the orders of your king?" he asked. "Did you not know that offerings to the goddess of war were required of every citizen of Jericho?"

"I did know it," Rahab said. She tried to think of a way to spin her words to get herself out of this. But she could not see how she could. Penzer knew she had not made her offering, and further, he knew she had turned him down. There would be no getting out of this except to tell the truth.

"Were you not aware that our city is under attack by a foreign enemy?" the king asked.

"I was, your grace."

"And yet you did not make your offerings to the goddess of war? To the one who has protected our city each day?"

"I did not." This time, her voice was loud and clear, and could no doubt be heard throughout the room.

"And why did you not follow the orders of your king?"

Rahab did not answer for a moment. She knew she had a choice to make, and that her decision would change everything. But she found that in this moment, she could not do anything but tell the truth. It may cost her everything, but she would not be silent.

"It is because I do not believe in the goddess Ashtart," she said. "I do not believe she has the power to save this city."

The room had gone completely silent. Even the sound of the guards breathing seemed to have stilled. The king's face changed, but he did not look angry, exactly. He seemed more... Well, truthfully, he seemed confused.

"What do you mean, the goddess does not have the power to save this city?"

Rahab took in a deep breath and then let it out slowly. It was too late now to do anything but continue down this path.

She could not take it back now. She thought of Salmon, of what he had told her about Yahweh. How He had led His people out of slavery and made them walk across the sea on dry land. How He had provided for them every day while they wandered through the wilderness. How He had led them to this land and had delivered their enemies to them, and they had not lost a single man. She remembered how Salmon had told her that his God had created the earth and everything in it. That He was their protector and redeemer. That He could be trusted.

"Yahweh is the one true God," Rahab said. "And He will prevail. All who trust in Him will be saved."

The room was no longer quiet. It erupted in shouts and gasps, in fear and confusion. But above it all, the king shouted, "Treason! That is treason!"

"Be that as it may, it is true," Rahab said.

Rahab did not hear the king give orders for her to be arrested and taken to the cells, but the guards did not waste any time in dragging her from the room and roughly shoving her down the stairs. Minesh was not among the guards who pushed her into the basement. These men pushed against her and called her names the whole way, telling her she would be dead before morning, but not until they each had a chance to torture her. She did not answer them and did not speak. She was led to a cell underground. The air was damp and musty, the ceiling low and covered in a thick black layer of grime. Prisoners in the surrounding cells called out to her as she passed, making lewd gestures and comments, before the guards chained her to the wall and shoved the gate closed behind her. The clang echoed in the dank space.

"Wait!" Rahab cried. "I must send a message!" Gibil. She would send a message to Gibil. He would help her. He would have to help her.

The guards laughed in return. She heard their chuckles echoing as they vanished down the hallway.

When the noise of the prisoners died down, Rahab looked around and took in her cell. The walls were damp and covered in most places in a layer of dark mold. The floor was mud, dotted with a few patches of hay. A bucket stood in the corner, out of her reach. The whole place stank of urine and other smells she did not care to think of. A man in another cell was moaning, and another was yanking on his chains, the sound filling the whole space with a constant grating sound.

Rahab found the chains were long enough that she could lower herself down to the floor. She eyed the filthy floor and remained standing.

What would she do now? What would happen to Salmon? To her family? What would happen to her? The guards had said that she would be tortured before she was executed, that she would be dead by daybreak. Could it be true? Surely there was a way out of this. But if there was not, if this was really how it ended for her—she hoped it would be quick.

What had she done? Why had she spoken up like that? Could she not have lied, have saved her own skin? More importantly, what would happen to her family now? Their one chance was to wait in Rahab's home when the Israelite army made their seventh march around the city. Now that Rahab was here in prison, would they be there? If she was dead, would they still come to her home and be protected by the scarlet cord? She feared she had doomed them all because of her impetuous words.

And yet, as she thought about it, Rahab knew she could have done nothing else. If she was given the chance to live those few moments in the throne room again, she would have done nothing differently. She knew the truth, and that truth had changed everything. Yahweh had changed everything. She could not hide it or downplay it. She could not do anything but share it.

No matter the cost.

CHAPTER NINETEEN

When the guards came back that night to slip a crust of stale bread through the bars of the gate, she tried again.

"I must get a message to my brother," Rahab said. The guard who had come this evening had several teeth missing and a slash across his cheek from some long-ago knife fight. "Please, take a message to him."

"Lady, I'm not a messenger," he said. He tossed the bread on its metal plate down on the floor, and the sound echoed throughout the dungeon.

"My brother is Gibil. He is a close adviser to the king. Please, tell him where I am."

The guard laughed. "If he is a close adviser to the king, your brother knows exactly where you are. He knows where you are, and he has left you here anyway." He moved off, tossing bread into the cell across the way, when the man in the next cell started to laugh.

"I did not realize we had ourselves a fancy lady," he said. Rahab could not see him, but his voice was high and muddled, as if he were speaking around a mouthful of pebbles. "Her brother knows the king and is going to come save her."

"Maybe he'll save us all," called another man on the far side of him.

Now the man in the cell directly across from Rahab chimed in. "Like the guard said, if she knew someone close with the king, she would not be here. That or he does not care."

There was laughter from down the hallway, and several other men chimed in with their opinions at once.

"Do not listen to them." There was a soft voice coming from the cell on the other side of Rahab. The man sounded old, but it was hard to say. "They are being cruel. This place does that to you."

Before Rahab could answer, the guard pounded on a metal bar with a club of some kind, and the men settled down. How many were in this prison? Rahab could not tell.

More importantly, how would she get out? Would Gibil advocate on her behalf? Would he be able to get her out? Did he even have that power? And would he use it if he did? Her relationship with her brother had been rocky, at best, and she had grown closer to Nuesh and Sagma. They were kinder, and they did not care so much about what people thought of them. They helped her when they could. They had not written her off when the truth of how she'd managed to pay down Mashda's debts became known.

Still, Gibil was blood. He would work to free her. He had to. If he did not—

But he would. The alternative was unthinkable. She could not stay here. Today was the fourth day of the Israelites' march. She needed to be home by the seventh day, to have gathered her family around her in the room with the scarlet cord, or all would be lost.

She found the cleanest place in the cell and sat down to eat her bread. It was tough, and spots of mold had already begun to appear on it. She ate it anyway, not knowing when she would have more. As she ate, she remembered Salmon's words. *If you only believe, you will see the glory of God.*

Rahab believed. She would hold on to hope that Yahweh knew where she was, even now. That He would find a way to get her out of this mess. But as the hours passed and night fell, it became harder and harder to hold on to hope.

A deep darkness descended on the basement jail as soon as the sun went down. There were no lamps or torches down here, and it was impossible to see even to the far side of her cell. She wondered what rats and bugs would scurry across the floor now that they could not be seen. She could find no comfortable position, and with her arms still chained to the wall, she had few options. The floor was filthy and smelled dank, and the men in the cells around her did not quiet throughout much of the night. How was a person to survive in a place like this? Rahab did not know. Eventually, around dawn, she finally fell into a fitful sleep, and she dreamed of the child she had lost. In her dreams, she held him in her arms again and saw his lifeless face all over again.

Rahab was awakened by a pounding sound. She sat up quickly and was startled for a moment to see that she was in a cell. Slowly, the events of the previous day came back to her. The pounding continued, like a thousand hammers striking the ground. Around her, the men in the cells began to jeer and shout.

"It is the army," the kind man in the cell to her left said. "Making their march once again."

It took a moment for Rahab to understand that he referred to the Israelite army. They were making their way around the city walls, carrying the ark of the covenant, once more. The ground shook. It felt almost as if the walls would not stand. From this place, below the ground, it sounded far different that it had from up on the wall back at her home.

Her home. She bit her lip as she tried not to cry. What of Garza and Gishimar? Were they doing all right? Did they wonder where she had gone? Had Salmon come back last night? She hoped he had stayed away, had not risked the eyes of the guards on him once more.

As she listened, the pounding of the army's feet gave way to the sounds of trumpets, and Rahab saw in her mind the priests, blowing their horns before the ark as it made its slow loop around the city. Then, more footsteps, and then it all went quiet. It was the fifth day.

Rahab tried to keep despair from overcoming her, but it was hard. Time passed slowly down here. There was nothing to do but listen to the moaning of the man down the way and the rattling of chains whenever one of the prisoners moved. She wondered who these other prisoners were and what they were being held here for. She wondered how long she would be held here. Would she be executed? Would she be left here to rot? If she was to be killed, she wished they would just get it over with.

She could not imagine being here when the army invaded, when she would die along with the rest of the citizens of Jericho.

Each time the door at the far end of the hallway opened, Rahab lifted her head, hoping it was Gibil, coming to get her out of here. But it was only the guards, coming to distribute food, or what passed for food around here. In the morning, another stale crust of bread. Toward the end of the afternoon, a small bowl of lentils. That was all. Rahab's stomach groaned, and she felt weak with hunger and exhaustion by the end of the afternoon. Throughout the day, men groaned and called out and made noises Rahab could not block out, no matter how hard she tried.

Just before night fell, the door opened once more, and Rahab looked up at the footsteps that came down the hallway. Was it Gibil, finally come to get her out of here? The footsteps slowed and stopped outside of the gate of her cell. She looked up, but it was only another guard. He held a torch, but it did little to chase away the gathering gloom.

"Rahab?" the guard called in a whisper.

Wait. She looked again, squinting in the darkness. It sounded like Minesh. She scrambled to her feet and rushed to the gate. "Minesh?"

"They told me you were here." He curled his fingers around the bars. "I could not imagine you in a place like this. What have they done to you?"

There was tenderness in his voice, and it made tears spring to her eyes.

"Minesh, please, send a message to Gibil. Please ask him to get me out of here."

"I will do what I can," Minesh said. "They told me you were taken before the king. That you committed treason. That you swore allegiance to the Israelite god. Can it be true?"

Rahab did not know how to answer. She did not know what to say. Minesh had loved her once. He had known her heart like no one else. He knew she could not have turned to the other side without good reason, didn't he?

"I will explain it all, when I am free of here," Rahab said. "I will tell you what I have learned. You can come, bring your family on the seventh day. I will make sure they are safe. But first I need help to get out of this cell."

"The king is very angry. There is talk of a public execution," Minesh said quietly.

"Please, help me get me out of here," Rahab repeated. "I must be home by daybreak on the seventh day. You must be with me. Tell my brothers and sisters too. They do not understand, but they must be there by daybreak on the seventh day."

In the low light of the torch, she could see that Minesh was looking at her with something like pity in his eyes. He thought she was having delusions. He thought she did not know what she was talking about. "I will do what I can."

"Please, Minesh." She put her hand on the bar, curling her fingers around his. "I will explain it all. You have to believe me."

Minesh did not pull his hand away but kept her fingers curled around his. Then, slowly, sadly, he pulled them away.

"I will do what I can," he repeated, and then he walked off down the hallway, back the way he came. The door slammed shut behind him.

CHAPTER TWENTY

After Minesh left, the dungeon went dark. The light was gone from the sky. She lay down to try to sleep, but the ground was hard and damp, and the noises from the other cells only seemed to grow louder as she tried to settle down. She must have drifted off at some point, though, because she was woken once again by the thunderous sound of footsteps. The Israelite army was marching once again. The sixth day.

Rahab knew this would be the last time the Israelite army would march around the city peacefully. This was the last day before the city would fall, and everyone in it....

She could not bear to think it. And the only way everyone she loved would be safe was if they were in the room on the wall. But she was not there to bring them.

It was unthinkable. Her mother and father. Their relationship had not been perfect. Far from it. But they were blood, and she loved them all the same. She thought about jolly Nuesh and Sagma. They were so wrapped up in their work and their families, but they had always been kind to Rahab. She thought of Ri. Her oldest sister had not deigned to see Rahab in many years, but Rahab loved her despite this. And there was Gibil. Haughty, proud Gibil. Sweet Hili, dreaming of her marriage.

Little Ushi. They would all be destroyed, along with everyone else in the city.

What kind of god would allow such terrible destruction? Such bloodshed? Rahab did not understand why every person in the city would have to die. But any of the gods worshiped in Jericho would have directed the same, she knew. Being able to command a mighty army was a sign of a powerful god. And Yahweh was different. He commanded such things because He loved His people and had promised them a land of their own.

He loved His people—she believed that. But it was starting to seem as though He had left her here to die. She was not one of His people and never would be. She should not have thrown in her lot with this God. If she had offered her sacrifice to Ashtart, as instructed, at least she would not be chained to the wall of a dungeon right now. She would no doubt die when the Israelites took the city, but at least she would not die in a damp and stinky dungeon.

"Yahweh, remember me," she whispered. She knew it was silly. You did not talk to the gods. They did not listen to the prayers in the hearts of mere mortals. The gods were to be worshiped, offered sacrifices. And yet Rahab knew Yahweh was different. More powerful. More loving. Perhaps He really could hear her. Maybe she could earn His love too, someday.

The sound of the Israelites footsteps was deafening and shook the small cells, but when it passed, when the last Hebrew soldier had made his way around the wall of the city, the silence was too loud.

Around midday, the door at the end of the hallway opened, and she heard several sets of footsteps. The man who brought the food always came alone. Could it be? Had Gibil finally come for her? But she knew it was not the case when the door of a cell down the row clanked open. The man inside—Rahab could not see who it was and knew nothing of him in any case—cried out, somewhere between a groan and a moan, and then Rahab heard the sickening sound of metal on flesh. The prisoner screamed, and there was a struggle. The men in the cells around him began to cry out, and Rahab heard chains rattling, metal clasps unlocking. The man shrieked, the sound of flesh being struck again echoed, and he went silent. Then she heard what sounded like whispered arguing, and something was dragged out of the cell and into the long stone hallway. The men in the cells around him let them all know what had happened.

"He's dead!" someone cried out.

"They've killed him!" another man shouted.

Up and down the row, the prisoners rattled their chains and shouted, crying out at the jailers as they removed the body from the cell and dragged him down the hallway toward... Well, she did not know what. She was glad she could not see what had happened from here. Her stomach turned just thinking about it.

Rahab did not eat the stale bread and mushy beans she was offered that day. As the sun moved through the sky and the beams of the afternoon light filled the small window at the top of her cell, she did not see why she should. It did not matter anymore. Unless something changed, something big, this would be her last night on earth. The last night for all of them.

When the sun went down, she finally let herself cry. This was the end. The end of everything she knew. The end of everyone she knew. She was surprised to realize that she hated the thought of the end of her life. She had thought she cared only for the loss of the ones she loved, but as she faced down the last hours, she realized that she did not want to die. It had been a hard life, full of disappointment and shame and loss. It was not the life she would have chosen if she had had the option. But it was hers. Every day that Yahweh had allowed her upon the earth had been precious, she now saw.

Rahab did not think she would sleep that night, but she must have drifted off at some point, because she was wakened by the sound of the metal gate of her cell swinging open. She sat up, terrified. The cell was dark. She could see nothing.

"Who is it?" she cried.

"Shh." Gibil. Her brother had finally come for her!

"Please, you must stay quiet." A different voice. Rahab cold not see his face, but she recognized the sound. That was Minesh. Minesh had come back for her. And he had worked with Gibil to get her free. She could hardly believe it. "Just hold still."

As Minesh began to unlock the braces that kept her chained to the wall, Rahab heard another voice. One that surprised her most of all.

"We have come to get you out of here," said Salmon.

CHAPTER TWENTY-ONE

Rahab did not understand how Salmon—the Israelite soldier and spy, the most hated man in Jericho—had come alongside her brother and childhood sweetheart to rescue her from her cell in the dungeon under the king's palace, but she did not stop to ask now. Salmon was dressed in the uniform of a palace guard, just like Minesh. How could this happen? How could these three men possibly be here together? But she knew she could not stop and ask. She simply followed the three men as they walked, as quietly as possible, out of her cell. After being chained to the wall for so many days, Rahab's arms felt free and light, and she wanted to swing them around to try to get feeling back into her hands, but she did not. Her legs were weak, but Salmon supported her as she walked, quickly and quietly, with the three men. A few of the men inside the cells rattled their chains or called out, but most seemed to be asleep, and Rahab and her rescuers were able to make it down the hallway and out into another hallway without any incident.

Rahab did not know where they were headed. She had not come this way when she had been brought to the prison. None of the men carried a torch, but Minesh knew the way, and he led them down one more dark hallway and up a staircase before he led them out a heavy door.

The night was dark, the moon a sliver, but she blinked against the brightness as she stepped out into a small court-yard. They were at the back of the palace. The garden was just past that fence, and yet no guard stood before the door. Perhaps Minesh was the guard who should be there. Rahab did not know. The air felt fresh and clean after the dungeon, and she took in several deep breaths, but she was pulled along. Salmon held her up as they hurried to a cart hitched to a donkey parked by the wall. Minesh lifted a pile of blankets in the cart, and Gibil indicated that she should climb inside. Salmon helped her into the cart, and the men piled the blankets back on top of her. A moment later, the cart began to move. Who was driving the cart? Where were the others? Where were they taking her? Rahab could only lie still and wait as the wooden wheels bumped over the rutted stones on the streets.

She did not know how long they traveled the streets of Jericho. It felt like a very long time. It felt like they hit every divot in the road, bouncing over the stones. She would have bruises after this, but she knew to stay silent. These men had risked much to rescue her tonight. She would remain quiet and trust that they knew what they were doing. She had no idea whether it was still night or daybreak was coming.

After a long while, the wagon finally pulled to a stop, and she heard Gibil's voice.

"I have brought that load of bronze from the palace." It was Gibil. Her brother had been the one driving her, then.

"It is about time. We are running low." That sounded like Nuesh.

"It is not as much as last time. Their offerings are becoming less plentiful." Gibil again.

"Most people do not have enough valuables to make sacrifices six days in a row," said Sagma. Gibil had brought her to the foundry, then. "It is no wonder there is not much iron in this batch."

Rahab understood that this visit to the foundry was a cover. A trick, in case they had been followed from the palace. So Nuesh and Sagma were in on it too. Whatever had happened to get her out of prison, her whole family seemed to have been involved.

"And yet the king cannot expect us to make plates for armor out of nothing," Nuesh added.

"This will be enough to keep your hammers working for some time," Gibil said. "I will bring more when I have it."

Her brothers were speaking loudly, but they fell silent as their footsteps drew closer to the cart. And then someone lifted up the blankets. Rahab looked up and saw Nuesh looking down at her. He placed his finger to his lips, and next to him, Sagma was gesturing for her to climb out of the cart. Nuesh held out a hand, and he helped her out. Gibil had backed the cart inside the foundry, where they could not be seen from the outside. It was dark inside the unlit building, but out of the open door Rahab could see that the first light of dawn was beginning to brighten the sky.

"We must go the rest of the way on foot," Gibil said quietly. He reached into the cart and pulled out a traveling cloak with a hood. She had been lying on it. "Let us go, quickly." He reached out his hand and handed her the cloak. "Put this on.

191

We must hurry." As Rahab hurried to put on the cloak, he looked back and Nuesh and Sagma. "You will come as soon as we've gone?"

"We will follow shortly behind you," Sagma said.

Gibil nodded, and then he pulled up the hood of his cloak and gestured for Rahab to do the same. So their faces could not be seen, she understood. Then Gibil started off, and Rahab walked just a step behind him, rushing through the dark streets of the quiet city.

"Where are we going?" Rahab whispered as they turned a corner and headed into the center of the city again.

"I do not want to go past the city gate," Gibil said, as if that explained everything. She understood that he was leading them circuitously so as to avoid the gate, but he had not answered her question.

"But where are we headed?"

Instead of answering he shushed her, and they continued to rush through the streets, staying in the shadows as much as possible. It did not take long for her to understand. She recognized this section of town. She knew these streets. And there could only be one destination in this part of town. Fingers of light streaked the sky, quickly turning from dark gray to a deep blue.

Rahab did not understand it, but she was not surprised when they stopped outside her own door. They climbed the steps quickly. Gibil knocked, three times quickly, and the door opened. Gibil shoved her inside.

When Rahab stepped inside the door of her home, she could not believe what she saw.

CHAPTER TWENTY-TWO

Rahab blinked. It could not be. How could this be possible?

"You are here." Kishar rushed forward and pulled Rahab toward her. What was her sister doing here? Rahab let herself be pulled into a hug.

"Just in time too," Gibil said.

The door slammed shut behind her, and when Kishar pulled away, she saw that Abu-Waqar stood on one side of the door, and Kishar's sons Awil-Ili and Sagar on the other. They bolted the door, not with her typical wooden beam but with a bar of iron.

"Took you long enough."

"Slowpokes." That was from her brothers Nuesh and Sagma. Somehow they had beaten Rahab and Gibil here.

"We had to go the long way, so we did not pass the city gates," Gibil said.

"It does not matter. We are all here now," Kishar said.

And Rahab turned back to the center of the room and saw that Kishar was right. They were all here. Hili stood to the side with Ushi in her arms. Gal stood next to her. Rahab's mother and father were here, seated at her table, along with their servants, who stood by the walls. Nuesh and Sagma had sent their

193

families ahead, and their wives and children were gathered in the corner of the room. Gibil had fallen into the arms of his wife, Erish, and his grown daughter and son had brought their families. Even her oldest sister Ri was here, alongside her husband, Hirin, and children. Rahab had not seen her niece Zelah since she was a child. Now she sat on the bench at the table next to Mama and Father, her belly swollen. And Garza and Gishimar sat by the window, looking out, next to Minesh, still in his guard uniform.

"How...?"

She did not even realize she was crying, but she found she could not get the words out. She did not understand. Aside from Kishar the other night, not one member of her family had ever set foot inside this house. None of them had ever dared risk the stigma of being seen here, in the home of...in her home. And yet tonight, on the night that mattered more than any other, here they were.

"What happened?" she asked. "How are you all here?"

Kishar took her hands and led her forward, gesturing for two of Gibil's daughters to move aside so there was room for Rahab on the bench by the table. The teenage girls—Hedu and Gedri—hopped up, and Rahab sat down on the bench. Someone—she did not even know who—put a cup of wine into her hands. Someone had brought plates of cheese and dishes of nuts and grapes, and there were many jugs of wine. It was a spread fit for a party, only this was a party of a very different sort.

The only one who was not here was Salmon. He would be with the Israelite army, she supposed. The army that was already making its way across the desert toward the walls of Jericho, she saw through the open window.

She looked around again. No, he was not the only one missing. "We must get Munzur," she said.

"Who?" Rahab's father wrinkled his brow.

"The beggar at the city gate," Rahab said. "He must be here too."

"We cannot go out and get him now," Gibil said. "Not when we have finally gotten you to safety."

"Then I will get him myself." Rahab started to push herself up.

"No, wait." Nuesh lunged toward her. "Rahab. So many have risked so much this night to keep you safe. We cannot risk more to get...to get this beggar no one knows."

"I know him." Rahab's tone was defiant. "Few would give him the time of day, but I always spoke with him. He is my friend. Truthfully, there is not so much difference between him and me. There was a time when I thought I would end up living on the street, begging for bread, just as he does. I also did not have any family willing to help me or a way to pay my bills. The only difference between me and Munzur is that I had something left to sell."

A loud silence followed her words. She did not care that she had just shocked them all. She had simply spoken aloud the thing they all knew to be true.

"I will not leave him to die," Rahab said, starting for the door.

For a moment, no one seemed to know what to do. Then, Sagma sighed.

"You cannot go out, Rahab. It is far too dangerous."

"We will go." Sagar, Kishar's son, had spoken. "Awil-Ili and I will go get the beggar and bring him here."

Abu-Waqar looked like he was about to argue, then thought the better of it. "You must be quick," he said, nodding.

Sagar and Awil-Ili unlatched the door and rushed out, and Nuesh and Sagma replaced the iron bar and stood guard.

"Thank you," Rahab said. She sat back down on the bench. "Now, can someone please tell me what happened? How did you all end up here today?"

"It was Kishar," Mama said. "She convinced us all we had to come."

"She told us it would be suicide not to," Father added.

"She told us you were right," Gibil said softly. "That you had been right all along. The Israelite army will advance on the city this day, and they will not be defeated."

"But—" Rahab could not get her mind around what they were saying. She was so very glad they were here, but she still did not understand. "But how were you convinced?" She turned to Kishar, who stood with Abu-Waqar next to her. "What made you change your mind? Last I saw you, you intended to turn me in."

"I was never going to turn you in." Kishar stepped forward and sat down next to Rahab on the bench. Rahab scooted over to make room her sister. "I was shocked and very scared for you. For all of us. But I found I could not turn you in."

"She risked everything by not telling me what she knew," Abu-Waqar said.

"I know she did," Rahab said. "And I am grateful."

"I thought you were a complete idiot. I thought you were careless and stupid and had put us all at risk," Kishar said.

"She was right," Nuesh added. "You are a complete idiot. That was a risky and foolish thing to do."

"And you did put as all at risk," Sagma added from beside his twin.

"But then I started to think about how you'd come to ask us all to stay with you on the seventh day. How you'd promised it was the only way we'd be safe," Kishar said. "And when I understood that you had been meeting with a soldier from their army, I began to realize that what you were telling us was not simply fanciful nonsense. I began to understand that what you were telling us was inside information from the mouth of the enemy."

"You did not turn me in when you met Salmon," Rahab said. She felt silly repeating what she had already said, but she was still trying to make sense of it. "Instead, you began to believe me."

"I saw that he had told you what would happen," Kishar said.

"She understood that you knew their plans," Gibil said. "And that you had tried to save us all with that knowledge."

"So I came back here the next night," Kishar said. "I knew you had been arrested, but I suspected Salmon did not know that. And I knew he had been coming here nightly, so I came here and waited for him."

"You came here and waited for Salmon?" Rahab repeated the words her sister had said, trying to get them to make sense, but they did not. None of this made any sense.

"I wanted to find out what he knew. What he would tell me. So I sat right here and waited, and sure enough, after nightfall, he climbed up the rope and swung his leg over the windowsill and climbed right in. I think he was quite surprised to see me." Kishar took a sip of wine from her cup and smiled.

"But how did you get in?"

"Your guest let me in." Kishar nodded at Garza, still seated by the window.

"I did not know what had happened to you," Garza said from the far side of the room. He looked pale and had dark circles under his eyes. "You went out in the morning and never came back. I did not know what to do, so I barricaded myself and Gishimar inside the inn." Garza seemed overwhelmed to be surrounded by so many of Rahab's relatives, or maybe it was just the situation that had him rattled.

"That was the right thing to do," Rahab said.

"So when this woman came pounding at the door, claiming she was your sister, I opened the door, hoping for news." Garza nodded. "She told me that you had been arrested and were in prison for treason. I did not know what to do."

"I did not give him a choice, in truth," Kishar said. "I pushed my way inside and bolted the door behind me, and that was that."

"My wife has a way of getting what she wants," Abu-Waqar said. A few members of the family laughed.

"Your guests went up to bed, and I waited," Kishar said. "And then your friend Salmon came in through the window, and I gave him the news that you had been arrested. He was very upset and insisted we must get you out. He went on and on about how you needed to be here on the morning of the seventh day. And then he told me why."

"I had sworn an oath," Rahab said. "I was not free to tell you what I knew. All I was able to do was beg you to come."

"None of us believed you," Gibil said.

"We did not understand that you had information that came directly from the spies," Nuesh said.

She could hear them now, thousands of footsteps as they marched, two by two, toward Jericho one last time. From here, she could see their armor glinting in the early-morning sunlight.

"I would have told you if I could have," Rahab said.

"We understand now," Father said. "And we thank you for trying to make us see. You could have kept that information to yourself. You did not have to try to save your family, and yet you did."

"You would have been justified in not helping us, considering how you have been treated." That came from Ri. Rahab was surprised to hear the words from anyone but especially from her. It wasn't an apology, but it was close. It was more than Rahab had ever thought she would hear from her sister.

"When Salmon told me what was planned, I knew it was true," Kishar said.

"I am surprised he told you," Rahab said.

"I do not think he would have, had it just been to save your family," Kishar said. "But it was when he found out you were in prison that he revealed to me the importance of making sure you were here on the morning of the seventh day. He had to tell me the plan of the Israelites so I would make sure to get you freed in time. He told me that only those who were in the house marked by the scarlet cord would be saved when they took the city. He revealed their army's plans, risking everything, to save you."

Rahab heard the sound of trumpets now, softly, off in the distance. The priests were on their way, carrying the ark of the covenant.

"You could have taken that information directly to the king," Rahab said. "You could have told the king exactly what the Israelites had planned, and King Uz would have rewarded you richly. Why did you not?"

"Why did I not?" Kishar laughed. "What good would it have done? What is the point in making myself rich, only to be killed two days later? What was clear to me, when I spoke with Salmon, was that it did not matter what Jericho's army did to try to stop them. The God of the Israelites would deliver Jericho into their hands, one way or another. There would be no stopping it."

"We have all heard of how they took the kingdoms of Sihon and Og," Gibil said. "Completely wiping out every person."

"Our army is strong," Abu-Waqar said, affronted.

"But not strong enough to stand against the power of their God," Gibil said. "The king believed the sacrifices to the goddess Ashtart would keep their army at bay. But many of us suspected they were simply biding their time. When Kishar told me what she had learned, I understood that they were indeed waiting and would advance on the seventh day."

"I told Gibby we needed to get you out," Kishar said. "He started to work on a plan right away. I worked on convincing the members of our family to come here tonight. I do not know which one of us had a harder task."

"In our defense, what you came to us saying, about a scarlet cord and a window and the spies, made no sense." That was Ri, from her perch in the corner.

"I know it did not," Kishar said. "But I had to make you see that it was true."

"Your sister can be very convincing," Hirin, Ri's husband, said, sitting next to his wife.

Just then, a knock sounded on the door. Three quick raps. "It is Sagar," called a voice from the other side.

Nuesh and Sagma unbolted the door and opened it, and a moment later, Rahab's nephews stepped inside, carrying Munzur between them.

"So it is true," Munzur said as they brought him inside. Nuesh and Sagma quickly latched the door again. "You have brought me to see Rahab after all." He looked around, his eyes wide.

"He put up quite a fight at first," Sagar said, setting the man down. Erish, Gibil's wife, hurried over with a mat to set him down on.

"I am stronger than I look," said Munzur. It sounded, as always, like he was speaking around some object in his mouth.

"He knocked me right in the eye," said Awil-Ili.

"But we finally convinced him that we were bringing him to you, and he quit fighting," said Sagar.

"They have not yet explained what this is all about," Munzur said, though he seemed content enough to be indoors.

"Thank you," Rahab said to her nephews. "You risked much, and I am grateful." She turned to Munzur. "The Israelites are coming. You will be safe here."

Munzur looked around, wary, but he did not say anything.

"You were telling me how you managed to convince the rest of the family to be here this night," Rahab said to Kishar.

"It took some doing," Kishar said with a nod. "What matters is that eventually, they all promised to meet me here tonight. I was finally able to convince everyone that what you have tried to tell them, Rahab, was right." She ducked her head at Rahab.

"Meanwhile, I was working on getting you out of prison," Gibil said. "It took longer than I had hoped to pull it together. Luckily, Minesh was game to help. I am sorry we could not get you sooner, but we worked as quickly as we could."

"And Salmon? How did he end up at the prison tonight?" she asked.

Rahab still did not understand how Salmon had been walking around the city as if he were just another man from Jericho and not part of the attacking army. The army that even now had reached the city gates and begun its long, slow march around the city wall. It would not be long now. They must hurry if Rahab was to get the full story.

"He insisted," Kishar said. "He planned it with these two the next night, here in this room." Kishar gestured at her brother and Minesh. "They all met here the night after I told him you had been arrested—"

"Honestly, I do not know if I would have believed it if I had not met him myself," said Minesh. "When I saw that he was real, truly a member of the army, and truly risking everything to save you, I knew I could do no less."

"It was the same for me," Nuesh said. "I wanted to free you, as quickly as possible, but it was when Salmon told us what was planned that I knew we had no time to waste."

Rahab tried to imagine it and could not. Salmon had met with Minesh and her brothers—Gibil, Nuesh, Sagma, all of them—here in her home. In the rooms they had not deigned to set foot in before. Enemies, all meeting to work together to save her.

"And you let him come along?" Rahab asked, still trying to get the pieces to fit together in her mind.

"Salmon said he needed to be there himself. To see it with his own eyes, that you were freed," Minesh said.

"And that was allowed?" Rahab still did not see how it was possible.

"He did not ask whether it was allowed," Gibil said. "He simply promised to show up again after nightfall yesterday, and he did so. I helped him in through the window, and he made his way to the prison. He said he knew where it was, from the time he was here before."

The time he and Ronen had been here to spy out the land, he meant. The time Rahab had met them and hidden them from the guards, including Abu-Waqar. It was amazing how much things had changed since that time just a few weeks ago.

"I met him at the side of the palace tonight and provided him the uniform of a guard," Gibil said. "He walked with me to the dungeon, where Minesh was waiting. But we did not have the key to the cell."

"Only the head guard has that," Minesh said.

"And you were not able to get it?" Rahab asked. Gibil had always made it sound as if he had nearly as much authority as the king himself. Surely the guards would listen to him.

"The head guard is only allowed to hand over the key on orders of the king himself," Minesh said.

"It was a very good thing Salmon was with us, in the end," Gibil said. Rahab tried to picture Salmon, the Israelite spy, creeping the hallways of the palace alongside her brother, his sworn enemy. It was too fantastical to be believed, and yet it was true. These truly were extraordinary times. "Salmon knew how to…eliminate the head guard."

Rahab shuddered, thinking about it. He had killed the man, to save her? That was terrible, it was wrong. And yet… And yet he had only died a few hours before his inevitable death anyway, by the hands of the Israelite army. Her ideas of what was right and what was wrong were becoming more and more confused. Her head spun, trying to make sense of it all. Somehow over the course of the last few days, she had come to simply accept that they were really contemplating the wholesale slaughter of the people of this town. How had she ceased to recoil from the very idea? Was she losing her grip on who she was?

"Salmon risked much to make sure you were safe," Minesh said quietly.

"I think he cares very much for you," Gibil added.

Rahab started to answer, but her words were swept up in the sound of bells ringing, of voices shouting.

"That will be the king's guard," Minesh said quickly. "They will have found the guard's body and the empty cell."

"They are announcing that a prisoner has escaped," Gibil added. "It will not be long before they come here, looking for you." He glanced at the window. "How close are they to finishing the circle around the city?"

"The last of the Israelites has vanished around the corner," Garza said from his perch by the window. "But instead of heading back toward their camp, they are marching again toward the city gate."

"That is good," Father said. "Then they will begin their assault soon."

"Hopefully before the king's men reach us here," Gibil said. Still, he stood and checked the bolt on the door.

"Wait," Garza said. "They are going around again."

"What do you mean?" Rahab asked. She stood and moved toward the window, as did her brothers. She saw that the scarlet cord was still firmly tied to the metal loop and draped out the open window. When she looked out, she saw that Garza was right. The soldiers in the lead were not stopping in front of the gates, as Rahab had assumed they would. Instead, they continued marching, as if they were going around the walls a second time.

"What are they doing?" Ri asked.

"Why are they going around again?" Mama craned her neck to look out the window.

"I hope they hurry up this time around," Nuesh said. "Those bells are getting closer."

Rahab saw the fear on his face, and she looked around at the faces of everyone in the room. They were all here. All the people she loved. She had not dared dream they would show up like this, and yet here they all were. Safe.

She knew that Abu-Waqar and Sagar and Awil-Ili were supposed to be lined up with the soldiers along the walls. Minesh had abandoned his post guarding the prison. Gibil was meant to be at the king's side. If they were caught here, it would mean death for them all. She understood what they all had risked to be here. What would it cost them if she was wrong?

But she also knew that she was not wrong. She knew, with every fiber of her being, that what Salmon had told her would happen would indeed come to pass. She knew that Salmon could be trusted. That Yahweh could be trusted. That He always kept His promises. That He would deliver His people. And that, because of His faithfulness, they would all be saved.

She felt joy, true joy, for the first time in a long time.

Then, the sound of bells and the shouting drew closer. The guards were shouting, "Prisoner escape! Prisoner escape!"

A moment later, there was a pounding at the door, and the room fell silent.

CHAPTER TWENTY-THREE

"**D**o not move," Gibil whispered, and everyone sat still.
"What if it is someone coming to look for refuge?"
Awil-Ili asked, but Gibil shook his head.

"Everyone who knew about the plan is here," he said.
"Those are the guards, looking for the escaped prisoner."

Looking for her. Looking for Rahab.

Rahab froze, and someone pounded on the door again.
"Open up!"

Again, no one moved. If the guards found them here, they
would be in grave danger. Surely they would all be killed.

"There is no answer," called the guard.

"She is in there. Try again," another one called.

The pounding on the door continued. "Open this door, by
order of the king."

"Why would she go back to her own home?" asked the first
guard. "She would know that is the first place we would look."

"Where else would she go?" called the other. "No one wants
someone like her inside their home."

"Try pushing the door open," called a third guard. The
guards began to ram the door, and though it creaked on its
hinges, the iron bar held it in place. But for how long? Could

they keep the men outside long enough for the Israelites to complete their next trip around the city walls?

The guards pushed and pulled at the doors, but they did not give.

"We will go back and get an axe," one of the guards said. "We will find her."

Slowly, the guards moved off, and Rahab let out a breath. They were gone, but for how long?

"We must reinforce the lock," Nuesh said, and he and his brothers and brothers-in-law moved toward the door. Some of them pushed her cooking table, and others gestured for them all to get up, and began pushing the table and chairs against the doors. At some point, Rahab heard the sound of the priests go past the window again.

"They are going around again," Garza said.

"What?" Rahab could not believe it, but when she looked out the window, she saw it was true. The army still marched, two by two, around the walls of the city, and those in the lead were beginning their third loop around. "They are marching around the city a third time?" Why would they do such a thing?

"Let's get the women and children upstairs," Abu-Waqar said, and Rahab immediately saw the wisdom of his words. The guards would come back. They would do whatever it took to get inside the house. Those inside needed to hold them off long enough for…long enough for the Israelites to do whatever it was they were going to do.

"Gather in the bedrooms, if you wish," Rahab said.

Erish gathered up her children, as did the wives of Nuesh and Sagma, and Hili took her younger cousins up the stairs. Kishar went as well, as did Mama, and soon it was only the men who were left on the main floor. The men and Rahab.

"You go up too, Rahab," Gibil said.

"No." She shook her head. "It is my fault the guards are at the door. I'll stay and help fight them off."

The guards came back just as the Israelites were beginning their fifth loop around the city. The sun had risen high into the sky by this point, and the day had turned hot. The air in the house was still and felt stifling with the thick tension. How many laps around the city would the Israelites take? What would happen when they finished? Would they be able to keep the guards away until that point?

"They are back." Hili's betrothed, Gal, was stationed by the door, his ear against the thick wood.

"Open up." Fists pounded on the door. "Open these doors by the order of the king."

Nuesh stood to one side of the door, Sagma on the other, swords raised. Gibil, Minesh, and Abu-Waqar braced themselves against the furniture that was piled against the door. They could not let them in. Rahab knew that if the guards entered the house, they would kill her. They would kill them all. They just needed to keep them out until the Israelites… She did not know. Until Yahweh did whatever He was going to do. The dull thudding of their footsteps hitting the ground again and again in a never-ending loop was making the whole city shake.

"Open these doors!" It was a different guard this time. "We are here for the prisoner Rahab, by order of the king!"

"We want the traitor!" called another voice.

"Send us the harlot!"

How many of them were there?

When there was no response this time, the guards did not wait. A sickening, splintering sound split the air. The door shook. They were using an axe to break open the door.

"Surely these men have better things to do than hunt for a poor woman," Gibil said under his breath. "There is an army besieging the city. Why are they not focusing on that?"

Another pounding sound. The groaning of ancient timbers, splitting under the sharp blade. They would not be able to hold them.

"We cannot hold them back. We must distract them somehow," Hirin, Ri's husband, said. Rahab had always thought him quite dull, but she saw the wisdom of his words now.

"Perhaps if I went to the roof, and called to them there," Rahab suggested.

"That will only make them try harder to get inside, if they know you are here for sure." Gibil winced as the axe hit the wood of the door once again. "They do not know you are here for sure, and look what lengths they are willing to go to get inside."

Rahab tried to think. What would get these men to step away from her door now? They needed a way to focus their attention elsewhere.

The roof. If she went to the roof...

"I have an idea!" She turned and ran to the stairs, climbing them two at a time.

"Rahab!" Nuesh and Sagma followed after her. "What are you thinking?"

"I will distract them," Rahab said. "Mislead them." Her sisters' and nieces' faces pressed their way out of the doorways on the second floor as she passed, but she did not stop. Rahab ran past them and scrambled up the ladder to the roof. The door was sticking again, so she used her shoulder to press up against it, and she was able to lift it up. She climbed out on to the roof and quickly scrambled across the roof to the side, staying back from the front edge so those on the street could not see her. She climbed carefully over the rim of her roof onto the roof of the house next door and then the house beyond that. Rahab could hear the trumpets from the west side of the town. The priests were making their way around the city, in the middle of the army. How many times would they walk around these walls?

Rahab did not stop on this roof, but scrambled across the next. Her brothers followed behind her, keeping her in their sights but did not call out to her or stop her. Farther down the wall, at the gate and inside the parapets, guards were stationed, hurling down insults and arrows at the Israelite army, but this section of the wall was not guarded. Rahab picked her way across several more roofs and found her way to the roof of the deserted home at the end of the row. The roof was sagging, the mud peeling back in some places. She could see clear to the beams in several spots. Carefully, Rahab made her way to the front of the roof. The guards were still there, down on the street in front of her door, hacking at the battered wood with the axe.

"Hey!" she cried. "I'm over here!"

The guards on the ground looked up. One of them pointed at her, and another cried out. They left the front door of her house and rushed toward the door of the deserted home.

"Let's go," she called, gesturing to her brothers to follow her back to her house.

"Wait." Sagma had stopped, standing on the door that would open to the floor below. He pulled a small ampoule of liquid from his belt, and when Nuesh saw it, he laughed.

"Hurry!" Rahab called. Even now she could hear the guards making their way up the stairs inside the abandoned house. But Nuesh stopped next to his twin.

"Ingenious, brother." Nuesh knelt down and pulled a piece of flint and a curved piece of metal out of his own belt.

"A smelter always has the tools to make fire," Sagma said, sprinkling some of the clear liquid into a small puddle on a bundle of flax someone had left to dry ages ago. It was brittle and dried—exactly what her brothers wanted. Sagma set the metal down and knocked it with the flint, once, twice. It did not take long for the resulting spark to catch, falling into the liquid and flaming up.

"What if they are burned?" Rahab wanted to stop them but not hurt them.

"Their armor will protect them," Sagma said. "It is designed to do so."

"But the flames will keep them away long enough for the Israelites to get to them," Nuesh added. He blew on the flame gently, stoking the small fire. "More of the fluid," Nuesh said. Sagma sprayed the small flame with the flammable liquid, igniting the flax in a brilliant burst of flame. He quickly dropped the bundle of flax down onto the floor below and sprayed more of the flammable liquid so it spread. Then he pulled up the ladder, threw it down on the roof, and slammed the door shut.

"Now we run." Nuesh turned and rushed back across the roofs until they got to Rahab's once more. She looked down outside the walls again. The Israelite troops at the front of the army were leading the army around the corner and toward the north gate again. This would be their sixth time around the city. How many times would they make this trip?

The smell of smoke followed Rahab as she rushed over the rooftops and back to her own roof. She did not know whether the guards would turn back when they realized they could not make it to the roof or whether they would fight the flames to keep trying. In either case, she supposed her family would not be able to hold them back for long. But perhaps she had bought them some time. Back on her own roof, Sagma held up the hatch, and she scrambled down the ladder, with Nuesh just behind her. They closed and latched the door and then ran back, past the faces of her loved ones huddled in the upstairs rooms and down the steps to the first floor once again.

"Whatever you did, it distracted them," Abu-Waqar said.

"Rahab took them to the abandoned house and called to them from the roof," Nuesh said. "They went inside and began to rush up the steps. We took the ladder so they cannot get to the roof."

"They will be back soon, then," Minesh said. "We must not stop being vigilant."

"Is that smoke?" Gibil asked, sniffing.

"Yes." Nuesh smiled. "We made extra sure they will not get to the roof today."

"You set the house on fire?" Gibil's mouth hung open.

"Just the way to the roof." Sagma had drawn his sword again and was moving toward the door.

"What if the house burns?" Gibil asked. "What if the fire spreads?"

"It was not a big flame," Nuesh insisted. "It will not spread to this home."

"It had better not," Gibil said. "Or we are all lost."

"At least it has bought us some time," Rahab said. "Garza, what do you see?"

Garza called from his perch by the window. "They are going around again. This will be seven times."

Surely this had to be the last time. The sun was high in the sky. It had to be past midday. How long could they go in circles?

Moments later, the guards were back at Rahab's door. They did not ask her to open the door this time. They simply began using their tools to strike the door.

"You tried to burn us alive!" one called out.

"We will burn you when we get our hands on you," another echoed.

All the men inside the house braced themselves against the door or against the furniture piled against the door. The wood groaned as they pushed against it, but the iron bar held it in place. Rahab did not know what would happen once they broke apart the wood of the door. Why didn't Salmon and his army hurry?

The smell of smoke grew stronger. Had the fire spread? Had setting it been a mistake? She did not know. She could only focus on the more immediate threat—the guards who were trying this very moment to break down her door. They needed to hold them off.

Yahweh, please show Your power now, she said in her mind. She knew gods did not care about the thoughts of the people who served them, but it had worked when she hid the spies, almost as if Yahweh had heard her. Almost as if He was a God who listened and cared. *Keep the guards out.*

She did not know how long they stood there, braced against the door, holding it closed against the king's guards, who tried with all their might to get inside. Each sickening thud of their axes made the door yield a bit more. Her brothers had their weapons drawn for when the door failed and the men rushed inside. They had to keep them out, just a little while longer.

"Something is different," Garza called from the window. "They're stopping."

"The army is stopping?" Abu-Waqar called.

"Yes. The ones in front have stopped in front of the city gate. The trumpeters are with him."

"They had better hurry," Gibil cried. "The door is splintering. We cannot hold them back much longer."

Rahab was not being much help anyway, so she left her place at the door, and she rushed to the window and stood next to Garza. She craned her neck to see what was happening. There was a man standing before the city gates. The one who had been in front. Their leader. Joshua. He was huge, muscled and stocky, but younger than she would have guessed. The priests with the trumpets and those carrying the ark of the covenant had moved up to the front and were standing just behind him. As Rahab watched, the priests blew the trumpets, making the same call that had become so familiar. And then, in the silence that followed, Joshua began to speak to his men.

"Shout!" he cried. His voice was deep and resonant, and it carried across the valley. "For the Lord has given you the city."

The soldiers began to cheer, but Joshua continued. "The city and all that is in it are to be devoted to the Lord. Only Rahab and all who are with her in her house shall be spared because she hid the spies we sent."

At the sound of this, the air inside the house immediately felt lighter. They would not be forgotten.

"But keep away from all the devoted things so that you will not bring about your own destruction by taking any of them. Otherwise you will make the camp of Israel liable to destruction and bring trouble on it. All the silver and gold and the articles of bronze and iron are sacred to the Lord and must go into His treasury."

The wood of her door splintered once more and with a groan, began to give. Rahab wished Joshua had given instruction to his men ahead of time. Why was he wasting time with such things now? But as he finished speaking, the trumpets sounded again, and all of the people of the army gave a great shout. They raised their voices as loud as they would go, crying out in victory. Their mouths were wide open, their faces contorted. The sound was deep and resonant, and echoed throughout the house. They shouted as if they were in pain, as if everything depended on how long and how loud they shouted. It was terrifying. It was exhilarating.

It was nothing compared to what came next.

When the men finished their primal scream, all of Jericho was eerily quiet. For a moment, all was still.

Then the rumbling began.

CHAPTER TWENTY-FOUR

Rahab did not know what was happening at first. The rumble she heard grew louder and louder, and the earth began to shake. The ground seemed to buckle underneath them.

Upstairs, the women and children cried out. What was going on? The whole earth was shaking. It felt like the very walls of her house were going to collapse around them.

Rahab rushed to the roof once again. She would be able to see what was happening from there. Her brothers and the other men followed after her. The whole house was still shaking when she emerged onto the roof.

She let out a cry as soon as she took in the scene.

Chunks of stone from the city wall had already begun to fall. Large sections of the wall toppled down as they watched. The men in the Israelite army had to scatter to avoid the falling rocks, which threatened to crush them. It was the first time Rahab had seen them break ranks. While she tried to make sense of it, more pieces of the city wall crumbled. The guards on the wall shouted as the wall disintegrated underneath their feet. Rahab gasped as she saw two guards fall from the parapet, the stones crashing down around them, and land with a sickening thud on the ground outside the gate. Their bodies were soon crushed as more chunks of stone and plaster fell.

"What is it?" Gibil came up behind her, followed by Minesh and her nephews

"Oh my," Nuesh muttered, and then even he and Sagma were silent as they took in what was happening.

It was not to be believed. It was almost as if—

"The very walls are coming down," Gibil said.

In the houses all around, Rahab heard screaming, but the sound was quickly swallowed by crashes and thuds. A large chunk slammed into two of the guards outside her door, and the others shouted and, leaving their swords behind, ran.

All around them, the city wall had fallen, stones tossed one from the other. The parapets at the corners were gone, the walls beneath turned to dust. The ramparts around the city gate too had vanished. Even the houses and businesses that butted up against the wall had collapsed. Piles of rubble lay in their place. The king's palace, perched high on the hill so it could be seen from all parts of the city, had partially collapsed from the shaking. On either side of Rahab's house were gaping holes where the buildings had collapsed, with their inhabitants inside of them. As far as the eye could see, Rahab's house was the only structure against the wall that stood. Everywhere else, the wall was gone.

And in the place where the wall had been, soldiers were streaming into the city.

Rahab began to weep. She could not believe it. Their beautiful city, turned to rubble. All around, she heard cries of terror and shrieks and moans.

"I must go help," she said, and started for the door in the roof again. "There are people hurting." But Gibil grabbed her.

"You must stay here," he said. "Only those inside these walls will be spared. You cannot leave."

Beneath them, Israelite soldiers streamed through the streets. She watched as two entered the house across the way, swords drawn, and heard a terrified scream, a low moan, and then silence. The soldiers rushed out of the house and into the next. Blood dripped from one of their swords. Soldiers swarmed the houses around her, but none entered her home. Rahab knew why. She knew that the house marked with the scarlet cord would be protected.

Rahab knew her brother was right, but it did not make it any easier to accept. She did not see how she could simply sit here while everyone around her was killed. While they stood, a small group of the king's soldiers rushed through the streets, but they were met by the Israelites and easily overpowered.

The Israelites would win this battle. There was no doubt in her mind that Jericho would fall this day and be delivered into the hands of the Israelites, just like the kingdoms of the Amorites before them. The city wall, which had stood against so many arrows and attacks over the years, had collapsed, brought down simply by the voices of the Israelites, calling out to the Lord.

Yahweh had indeed given the city to His people. If she had ever had any doubts that He was the one true God, she did not have them any longer. Only the God of the universe could have made such a thing happen. Only the true God of the universe could have caused her home to be spared, and her home alone.

He was powerful and mighty, and yet, this day, she knew beyond all doubt that He also kept His promises. That He knew her.

Dozens of Israelite soldiers were now storming the palace, swords drawn. She thought about the men in the prison beneath the sumptuous rooms of the king. None of them would be spared this day. The king, the guards, his wives and children… All would be lost.

"Let's go back inside," Gibil finally said. Rahab had never liked being told what to do by her older brother, but she saw the wisdom in his words now. It did no good to stay up here and watch everything they loved being destroyed. They would wait inside.

As she climbed down the ladder, Rahab saw the faces of her nieces in the doorways, and she realized that not everything she loved was being destroyed this day.

"We are safe," she called to Ri's daughters. The other women were still cowering in the sleeping rooms on the upper level.

"What is happening?" Mama stood in the doorway of one room, her mouth hanging open. Behind her, Kishar cradled Ushi in her arms, tears wetting her anxious face.

"Jericho is delivered into the hands of the Israelites," Rahab said. "But we are spared, just as Salmon promised. He kept his word. We are safe. Let us go downstairs and wait."

"Did the wall truly fall?" Olib, wife of Nuesh, asked.

"It has fallen," Father said.

"The only place the wall still stands is at this house," Gibil said. "Everywhere else, it has turned to rubble, and the soldiers are taking the city."

The look on the faces of her sisters and their children mimicked the difficult feelings roiling inside of Rahab. Terror mixed with disgust and shame. Relief that they had been spared. Gratitude that Kishar had believed her, had believed Salmon, and had gathered her family here in this house. Her brothers and sisters and mother and father were safe, because the one true God had recognized and kept His promises to His servant Rahab.

"I do not understand," Mama said, as Rahab helped her down the stairs back to the first floor to wait. "Who is this God Yahweh who has delivered His people this day? Is He truly more powerful than all the other gods?"

Despite everything, Rahab could not help but smile. "While we wait, I will tell you everything I know about Yahweh."

CHAPTER TWENTY-FIVE

As the day wore on, the sounds in the city around them stilled. Her brothers still stood by the door, swords drawn, ready in case anyone should try to attack this house the way they had taken so many others, but no one came. As the sun moved lower in the sky, the moaning and crying and screaming died down, and the sound of footsteps outside the door became less frantic, more intentional. Rahab tried her best not to think about what was happening all around her, in the market, at the palace. Was King Uz dead yet? Had the Israelites taken the palace? Or was that still to come? What had Penzer thought, when he understood he would not escape? She found she felt no joy in the knowledge of his death. Even he had not deserved this. She wondered what would happen to the temple, to all the sacrifices given to Ashtart and the other false gods. She wondered when King Uz had understood that his goddess of war was just a piece of ivory, an object that did not hold the power to save anything.

The horror of what was happening around them was still too much to bear. She could not let herself think about it. Instead, she focused on telling her family and friends everything she knew about Yahweh. About His covenant with Abraham to make His descendants as numerous as the stars in the sky. How He had led them out of slavery and made them walk across the Red Sea on dry land. How He had made a covenant with Moses and fed them as they wandered in the desert, and how, after the death of Moses, He had brought them across the Jordan River and given them this land as their homeland. There were many questions, most of which Rahab did not know how to answer, but she promised they would be able to ask the Israelites themselves soon. After what they had seen so far this day, none had any doubt that Yahweh was a God who could be trusted.

When she had finished telling them what she knew, Rahab's mother and father pulled her aside.

"I am sorry, Rahab," her mother said. "For how poorly you have been treated. By society, and by us." She paused and looked at her husband, who nodded. "Your father is sorry too."

Father did not say anything at first. Rahab realized she had not truly seen him in many years. His beard was mostly gray now, and his skin was spotted with age. His waist had thickened, his back curved, and his hands shook a little with every movement. He was an old man now, she realized. When had that happened?

Then he spoke too. "I am sorry for what you went through, Rahab. I know it was not... I know your marriage was not what it could have been, and your life since then has been difficult. I wish I could have done things differently."

It was not these things that had truly hurt Rahab the most over the years. The fact that her father had disavowed her and refused her the help she had needed had hurt more than she could ever express. The fact that he had not allowed her inside his home after she had done what needed to be done was more painful than she could say. And yet, despite it all, she could never stop loving him. She saw that now. No matter what happened, she would always love her mother and father, her brothers and sisters. No matter how they had treated her, her love for them had never wavered.

Mama and Father were not the only ones to express apologies to her in that afternoon. Gibil also pulled her aside.

"I have treated you very poorly, sister."

Rahab did not deny it.

"I judged you wrongly." He was right about that too, but she kept quiet, and he continued. "I did not understand that you were driven to desperation. At the time, all I could see was that you had sullied our family name. I know now that it was I who did that, by not helping you when I could have. By allowing you to be in a position in which your only choice was starvation or...what you did."

She felt tears well up, and she bit them back. She finally felt seen by her brother, by her family. She wished it had not taken saving them from certain death to get here, but she was not going to complain now.

"I thank you for loving me anyway. For saving me anyway, me and my family," Gibil said.

"None of us deserve the salvation that has been given to us this day," Rahab finally managed to say. "But for the love of Yahweh, none of us would stand."

It was nearing evening when the knock on the door finally came. All of the men drew their weapons, but then Salmon called out, "Rahab! It is Salmon and Ronen. It is safe for you to come out now."

The sound of his voice was like honey. She had not realized how much she had been waiting to hear it. She gestured for her brothers, nephews, and father to lower their weapons, and she unbarred the door and pulled it open.

Salmon was standing there, Ronen next to him. They were battered, their armor dented. Ronen's helmet was crushed, but both of them smiled at Rahab. They wore the armor of the enemy, but they had shown her mercy she had never received from the people of Jericho.

And they had come for her. They had spared Rahab and her family. They had kept their promise. She felt tears well up in her eyes.

Now that they were standing here, Rahab found she did not know what to say. She had so many questions, so much she did not understand, but the words would not come. She gazed at Salmon's handsome face, saw the way he was looking back at her, and she knew she would have plenty of time to ask questions later. For now, she had to get her family and loved ones out of here and into safety.

Salmon did not speak. He simply stepped forward and pulled her into his arms, pressing her against him. His arms were strong, and she felt herself sink into them. She realized this was what she had been waiting for all through the day. She never wanted to leave the safety of his arms. But after a moment, he pulled back, gazed at her, and said, "I am very glad to see you made it. Are you all right?"

"I am fine," Rahab said. "We are all safe."

"Looks like you've got a full house," Ronen said, looking around Rahab to the room behind her. His voice was somehow still jolly, just like always, in spite of all that had just happened. "You've got half of Jericho in here."

"These are just my family and friends," Rahab said.

"We are grateful to you for your protection," Father said, rising and walking toward the door.

"It is Rahab who has saved all of you," Salmon said. "Her quick thinking and her faithfulness are the reason any of you are still here today."

To hear it spoken aloud was almost more than she could bear.

"Come," Ronen said. "We must hurry. Joshua will give the signal shortly, and it will take us a while to get all of them out."

"He's right," Salmon said. He raised his voice. "We need to have everyone please gather their things quickly and follow us."

"You can put away your swords," Ronen said to Nuesh and Sagma. "You will not need them now."

Everyone in the room began moving at once, standing up, gathering their things. Nuesh and Sagma stood near the front, still keeping their swords drawn, while Erish and Olib guided their children toward the door, and Garza helped pregnant Zelah. Minesh held the arm of Mama, making sure she was steady on her feet. Sagar and Awil-Ili carried Munzur.

When they were all ready, Ronen led them out the door. "It is probably best to keep your eyes on the ground," Ronen said, and judging by the gasps Rahab heard as her nieces went out the door, he was right to do so. She could not imagine what the city looked like now. She would see it soon enough. For now, Rahab stood still and watched as the members of her family walked out the door of her home and into a new life, one none of them could imagine.

Salmon stood by the door, and when the last members of her family had gone, he gestured for her.

"It is time to go," he said.

Rahab nodded, but she stood still a moment longer, looking around the main room of the house that had brought her so much grief. The home where she had come as a bride, no more than a child, and lived with a man who treated her poorly. Where she had lost her baby, and all of her dreams along with them. Where she had seen Mashda pass, where she had been forced to rent out rooms and more to survive. It wasn't hers. It had never belonged to her. Yet it was all she had.

"I will never forget that first night in this room," Salmon said, coming up next to her. "I will never forget what I felt, talking to you that first time."

"You stood up for me." Rahab looked up at him now. She had forgotten how strong his jaw was, how smooth his cheeks. The golden flecks in his dark eyes.

"I had never met anyone like you." He reached out his hand and touched her arm gently. "All I wanted to do was be there beside you. That's still all I want."

Rahab let the touch of his hand steady her. Her heart was beating too fast, her emotions moving so quickly she could not make sense of them. All she knew was that she felt the same. She wanted to be beside Salmon all her days.

"You do not answer me," Salmon said. "Do not tell me you do not feel the same."

Rahab considered her words carefully. "I have never met anyone like you either," she said. "Most men…they do not see me for anything more than my reputation. You saw me for who I truly am."

Salmon moved his hand down her arm, slowly. "You are so much more than your reputation. You are so much more than your past. Your past does not matter to me, and it does not matter to Yahweh. He knows the number of hairs on your head, and He loves every part of you. And it is who you are today and what you have done that will be remembered."

Rahab smiled. He was kind. That was what she had first noticed about him. "You have always been kind to me."

"I am not just being kind, Rahab." He moved his hand down and took hers in his. Their hands clasped, and Rahab felt a warmth spread through her. "You will be remembered, Rahab. What you did for us, for the Lord—your bravery will be told throughout the land and your story passed down among the generations."

Rahab doubted it. "Who would ever care about the story of Rahab, the harlot?"

"That is not who you are, Rahab. That is not who you have ever been." He threaded his fingers through hers. She never wanted to pull her hand away. She wanted him to come closer.

"You are not defined by your past acts. You will be remembered as a righteous woman who fears the Lord."

"You two coming?" It was Ronen, shouting from the doorway. Salmon looked toward the door but did not pull his hand away. "Joshua's going to let them in with the torches soon. You need to get out of here."

"We should go." Salmon started walking toward the door, keeping her hand in his. "Is there anything you need to take?"

Rahab looked around one last time and shook her head. "There is nothing here I want."

"Then let's go." He led her to the door and through the doorway, and she stepped out into what used to be the street. Now, it was mostly a pile of rubble, slick with the dark stain of blood. A sharp metallic scent hung in the air. "Best to keep your eyes down."

But she looked anyway. She wanted to take it all in. Jericho was completely destroyed. There was not a house intact along the outside of the city, and the houses farther into the city were all standing open, blood running out their doors. The Lord had truly given this city into the hands of His people.

Salmon helped her pick her way over the stones and to the easiest place to cross over what used to be the wall. All along the outside of the wall, Israelite soldiers stood, burning torches held high.

Salmon stopped and went to talk to the one closest to the wall. She recognized the leader, Joshua. Up close she saw he had a neat beard and hawklike eyes.

"They are all out. You can send the men in," Salmon said to him. Joshua nodded, and he looked at Rahab and nodded at her as well.

"Thank you for all you have done, Rahab," Joshua said. "Your faithfulness will not be forgotten." And then he turned to his men and called out, "It is time. Burn it down."

Salmon pulled her forward so she did not have to see the soldiers rushing in to set fire to what remained of the city she had called home. She had no love for Jericho, but it was all she had ever known. She had a new home now, she knew. Wherever Salmon was, that was her home.

Ronen had caught up with her family and friends and was leading them across the plain toward the Israelite camp. Salmon led her along the same way.

She did not know what lay ahead. She did not know what her new life would look like. She didn't know whether they would be received into the Israelite camp, whether her family and friends would treat her differently now. She did not know what it meant to serve and worship Yahweh alone.

But she would find out. And she would never forget, as long as she lived, that His mercy and faithfulness had spared them all. That Yahweh was a God who could be trusted.

When they had walked for a while, Rahab started to turn back.

"You should not look back," Salmon said. "You probably do not want to see."

But she did want to see. She stopped and turned back and saw Jericho in flames. They danced and spun in the gathering evening, consuming everything she had ever known. From this distance, she saw clearly what she already knew to be true—she saw that the only part of the wall that remained was the house where she had lived. Even now, the scarlet cord hung from the window, fluttering in the wind. The scarlet cord—the color of blood—that had saved them all.

"Let us go," Salmon said, pulling her back. "We should get you to the camp before it gets too dark."

Rahab nodded, turning away from the burning city, and resumed walking toward the Israelite camp. She did not know what her life would look like now, but she knew she served the one true God and would follow wherever He led her. For now, that was enough.

Letter from
THE AUTHOR

Dear Reader,

I can't remember when I first heard Rahab's story. In its sanitized version (we never really talked about Rahab's past…) it is one of the stories repeated often in Sunday school. I knew that Rahab lived in the wall in Jericho, that she hid the Israelite spies, and that because of that and a scarlet cord she hung in her window, she and her family were saved when God delivered the city to the Israelites. I knew that, in the words of the African American spiritual, "the walls came tumbling down." The basic facts.

But I'd never stopped to question what would motivate Rahab to protect the spies—enemies, intent on capturing her city—and what it might have cost her to do so. I'd never considered what she was giving up by choosing to throw in her lot with the invading army or how she might have managed to gather her family in the room with the scarlet cord. I'd never asked about what it must have been like for Rahab to watch the only home she'd ever known be utterly destroyed, and to walk out of the ruined city and join a whole new tribe and family. I don't know how Rahab felt and what it must have been like for her, but in this book I've done my best to imagine it.

There are plenty of things we do know about Rahab, though. At the end of the biblical account of the conquest of Jericho, in Joshua chapter 6, we are told that "Joshua spared Rahab the prostitute, with her family and all who belonged to her, because she hid the men Joshua had sent as spies to Jericho— and she lives among the Israelites to this day" (Joshua 6:25 NIV). So we know Rahab must have walked out of the rubble and begun a new life with God's people. We also know that she is commended in the New Testament in James 2:25 and Hebrews 11:31 (in the passage sometimes referred to as the Hall of Faith) for her faithfulness and good works. Salmon is not kidding when he tells her in this story that she will be remembered for what she did for God's people. She is remembered even today for her courage and her faith.

Rahab is also mentioned in another New Testament passage, Matthew 1:5–6 NIV. There, Matthew is recounting the lineage of Christ, and among those mentioned in the list, we find, "Salmon the father of Boaz, whose mother was Rahab, Boaz the father of Obed, whose mother was Ruth, Obed the father of Jesse, and Jesse the father of King David." Because of her brave acts, Rahab not only saved herself and her family and became one of God's people, she—along with her husband Salmon—had the distinct honor of being one of the ancestors of King David and, eventually, Jesus Christ.

In my research for this book, I couldn't find any real information about who Salmon, husband to Rahab in this genealogy, was. The only places he's mentioned in Scripture are Ruth 4:20–21 and Matthew 1:4, where we learn his father was named

Nashon. He's certainly an Israelite, and he must have been one of the young men Rahab met once she'd joined the tribe of God's people. I don't have any evidence that Salmon was one of the spies who was protected by Rahab, but there is plenty of speculation that he might have been. I like to believe God brought the spy and his protector together in this way, but we'll probably never know for sure.

Whatever the truth is, Rahab's story reminds us about the incredible things that can happen when we put our trust in God, even when we don't understand His plans. He is faithful and can be trusted, even when things don't make sense. God cared for Rahab and was faithful to her, and He cares for us and protects us as well.

I hope you enjoyed reading this book as much as I enjoyed writing it.

Beth Adams

A SCHOLAR'S VIEW OF JERICHO

Rahab would not have much difficulty recognizing the terrain surrounding Jericho if she walked the hillsides today. Even though thousands of years have passed, the site of this ancient city has changed little.

As the Hebrews moved out of the desert, they moved into a land where agriculture and polytheism intertwined. Alluring goddesses personified fertility in crops, animals, and humans by making oven-baked frescos of gods like Astarte and Baal, the sun god. The Hebrews became the first people to fight and destroy these gods of nature.

But in ancient times, as today, men also fought against each other. Jericho first existed somewhere between 10,000 and 9000 BC, making Jericho possibly the oldest of most ancient cities. Palestine, better known as Canaan, was a collection of independent city states, with each city under the control of its own king. They needed massive defense walls because these independent city-state kings frequently attacked each other. The thick walls of Jericho from this time attest to that theory. Over the course of a six-hundred-year period, the walls of Jericho were rebuilt sixteen times.

Wars were not the only cause of destruction. Earthquakes, water in the foundations, and other natural causes played a role in the need for constant maintenance of the city defense structures. Outside attackers frequently raided the city, leaving evidence of fire and other damage. The people of this time developed technologically and culturally, but led lives of very little peace and much instability.

The location of Jericho has always been strategic. It was built on the site of a spring that still provides water for Jordan Valley gardens. In the arid territory covering a large area, a source of water remains forever vital.

Because of Jericho's position near the Jordan River, anyone coming from the Jordanian side would have to access this city in order to continue on into what is today Israel. While archeologists argue over some of the dates surrounding Jericho's history, most agree that by 9400 BC there were at least one to two thousand people living there.

Running close by is the "The King's Highway," the most ancient of highways that linked Mesopotamia with Egypt and traversed the Sinai Peninsula to Aqaba. Merchants used this road to sell goods in Transjordan, Damascus, and along the Euphrates River. In the most ancient of times, The King's Highway was the world's most important commercial route. Even invading armies generally respected this trade route and would avoid disrupting the flow of traffic. Because of the location of the mountains, the Jordan River, and adjoining valleys, Jericho remained all-important.

Rahab's world would have encompassed this terrain of the commercial route. While one cannot be clear about how far her knowledge of the area reached, she would have known about the

King's Highway and the great Jordan Valley. Her world would probably have been more sophisticated than one might have thought because of the flow of traffic from Mesopotamia to Egypt.

Some years ago, I was in Jericho and traveled up the King's Highway. I was amazed how precise and clear this ancient road-way still remains. The wide expanse almost appeared to have been established by modern road graders and bulldozers. As one traverses this path, off in the distance Jericho comes into view.

Much like the terrain of Southern California, the flat lands suddenly rise up into towering mountains that become the high desert. From one of those peaks, a visitor can look down on Jericho. In fact, Mount Nebo, where Moses had his first and last view of the Holy Land, is on the edge of his mountain range. I, too, stood on a cliff on Mount Nebo and realized that from that height I could see from the Sea of Galilee down to the Dead Sea and out to the Mediterranean. I will never forget the sight.

The Hebrews took this location into account as they strategically moved across the Jordan. By taking Og and Sihon first, they avoided destroying the trade route. The same was true when they turned their attention to Jericho. While one cannot clearly decipher militarily why they marched around the city for days and blew horns, it must have been painfully obvious to the residents of Jericho that they were following the Lord's commandments. A stern reminder indeed!

In the 1950s, famed archeologist Dame Kathleen Kenyon came to Jericho to dig for the remains of the fallen walls of the city. She placed the establishment of an agricultural economy at about 7000 BC. In addition, she uncovered a massive stone wall and a great tower of the same date. She also found elaborate domestic architecture from the seventh millennium. I looked into the giant hole where she had dug down to expose the walls of Jericho. The remains of the wall were impressive. She noted that she found no evidence of fallen city walls.

What do we make of the fact that an archeologist like Kenyon did not find physical proof of the walls falling? Some would say that the centuries have simply erased and blown away the remains. On the other hand, her work only touched one small area. The stone edges of the exposed section are impressive, but the dig is only about fifty feet wide at best. The depth is amazing, but it is only a small section. What Kenyon missed was that Jericho was built and rebuilt a multitude of times, and she simply touched on one edge of the ancient world.

What would Rahab have found if she had wandered through the marketplace in old Jericho? While offerings would be sparse by our standard, one can find an approximation in today's Old City in Jerusalem. With water from the spring, farmers cultivated vegetables and grains. I have seen in this market radishes as big as softballs and cabbages like a basketball. Obviously, the land of milk and honey had excellent fertility. Would Rahab have found vegetables of such size? No way of knowing today, but the fact that Jericho endured through eons of time bears testimony to agricultural productivity.

Like Jericho, Hebron was another city that stood out in ancient times. We first hear of Hebron in the book of Genesis when

Abraham acquires the Cave of Machpelah for a family burial site. Decades ago, I first visited the burial site of Abraham and his kin. The Cave is considered a holy place.

Hebron was to play an important part in the future history of Israel. After David fled from Saul, he settled in Hebron. For seven and a half years, David and his army lived there while the nation tried to reconstitute itself. A civil war ensued that finally resulted in the death of Abner, the opposing general, who was buried at Hebron. Finally, the elders of Israel gathered at Hebron, and David was crowned king.

As one approaches Hebron today, the city's architecture is distinctive. The old part of the city is built of white stone. The quarrying of limestone still constitutes a major portion of the city's commerce. Would Rahab recognize Hebron today? Probably not.

Fiction Author
BETH ADAMS

Beth Adams lives in Brooklyn, New York, with her husband and two young daughters. When she's not writing, she spends her time cleaning up after two devious cats and trying to find time to read.

Nonfiction Author
ROBERT L. WISE, Ph.D.

The Rev. Robert L. Wise, Ph.D., is the author of thirty-five books and numerous articles published in English, Spanish, Dutch, Chinese, Japanese, and German. On the internet he weekly publishes *Miracles Never Cease* and monthly presents live interviews on YouTube with people who have experienced divine interventions.

*Read on for a sneak peek of another exciting story in the
Extraordinary Women of the Bible series!*

A HARVEST OF GRACE:
RUTH AND NAOMI'S STORY

JENELLE HOVDE

The massive city gate of Kir-hareseth loomed in the gathering
twilight, the sharpened palisades on either side of the walls
like a row of jagged teeth, while a faint sickle—the moon—offered
only a dim light to illuminate the empty streets. Ruth arched her
neck to gaze at the sky, her heart pounding with an erratic rhythm.
The Moabite king had ordered the gate closed today, preventing
anyone from entering or leaving while a fever swept through the
poorest quarters. Above her, the pale moon sliced through the
black heavens as wisps of silver clouds fled. It was not a god, as
Ruth had been taught as a child. The story she had been told was
that Yarikh, whose dew watered blossoms in the desert, courted
his goddess at night. This evening, something felt evil about the
celestial body clinging to the dark expanse above.

She lowered her head and breathed a prayer to Yahweh,
just as her mother-in-law, Naomi, had taught her. *Please deliver
Mahlon from the fire eating him from within.* A strangled sound
broke free of her as she rushed into another darkened alley, a
shortcut leading to the physician's house. She clamped her

teeth tightly together, shaking her head to clear the image of her beloved husband lying helpless on a mat. Mahlon dying? It didn't seem possible.

What if she didn't find Takesh in time? Other healers had refused to come to her house, regardless of the coin offered. What if her husband passed...

No. She mustn't think such morbid thoughts. He would live and tease her as he always had.

"We need to hurry." Orpah's pained voice cut into Ruth's turbulent thoughts. Her sister-in-law panted as she jogged to keep up with Ruth's resumed pace. "We cannot be the only ones in need of Takesh's services."

Orpah, two years younger than Ruth, appeared haggard, with dark circles curving beneath her eyes. Her loose tunic, missing a belt, bore evidence of a hard day of work grinding grain, the flour still clinging to the folds, while Ruth had tended to her ill husband and brother-in-law. When Mahlon's eyes rolled back in his head, leaving only the white, Naomi had begged both women to find help. Not that she needed to ask Ruth. Ruth had already flung a light blue *miṭpaḥ*, a shawl, over her shoulders, desperation clawing within her to save her unconscious husband. Two women in the city at night provided scant protection for each other, but it was better than going alone.

She glanced down at her worn tunic, just as rumpled and stained as Orpah's. Did she bring sickness with her? She had no desire to hurt anyone, but neither could she let her husband suffer. Dust stirred beneath her leather sandals as she broke into a fresh run while ignoring the throb in her chest.

Don't leave me, Mahlon.

Ten years ago, he had found her hiding behind a perfume market stall, trembling, while another man, one who had assumed she would be his, stalked the rows of shops to find her and drag her home. A teasing glint appeared in Mahlon's eyes when he discovered her crouched on the ground, just as a vial of ointment tipped and fell from the table. His hand shot out and caught the alabaster flask, saving her the exorbitant cost of ruined perfume but not the mortification staining her cheeks.

"Is there a special perfume hidden beneath the table?" he asked with an amiable smile. A hot wind teased the unruly brown curls about his lean face. His brown eyes were warm and kind—a rarity, and far more precious to her than the most expensive of myrrh or frankincense.

Her chest fluttering, she ignored his good-natured teasing. "Is he gone? The thickset man who rushed past this table a moment ago?"

All at once, Mahlon sobered. He glanced over his shoulder before turning to her. "I see a fat man at the edge of the market. He turned left in the direction of the temples."

At the mention of Chemosh's temple, she shuddered to the point of her teeth chattering—even when Mahlon reached out a calloused palm for her to take. She felt his fingers wrap around her wrist, pulling her to her feet, just as the old seller spied her, a scowl plastered on his wrinkled face.

Four months later, following a horrible beating from her *abba*, Mahlon insisted on marrying her. To prove his affection, he placed a flask of bittersweet persimmon in her hand as a rare wedding gift. When she protested the cost of the perfume, he merely grinned. Persimmon was the scent of kings and queens, he told her. And he wanted to always remember the day he found her. With an abba who didn't care whether she lived or died, she had moved from a horrible home to one of peace and surprising joy.

Now peace was no more. She was about to lose the man she had grown to respect and love.

Ruth sucked in a pained breath, her lungs aching from running. She studied the exit of the narrow alley, trying to remember the crooked path to Takesh's mud-brick home. After several turns left, then right, she finally spied the large two-story house towering above the other buildings and darted forward. The sound of sandals slapping against the road indicated Orpah struggling to keep pace.

When Ruth reached the house, the walled gate remained locked. She raised her fist and banged on the weathered wood, the sound echoing in the night. A second time, she struck the door, and it swung open, revealing an old female servant, her stringy gray hair mussed. Defiant eyes held Ruth's gaze.

"Why do you bother Master Takesh's household at this late hour?"

Ruth swallowed, her mouth dry. "My husband and brother-in-law are dying with fever. Please, we need Takesh's help. Can he come with us?"

The old woman glowered, her lined face crumpling further like a shriveled date. "He is treating a nobleman's wife in the western district, and who can tell how long the delivery will take? Go home."

Orpah's cry of anguish matched the one reverberating in Ruth.

She sagged at the thought that there was no way to save Mahlon. Bracing herself against the wall, she tried again to invoke the servant's pity. "Is there no one who can help us? No other servant of Takesh who might bring herbs? We've tried every physician in the area, and we can't find a single healer."

Grimacing, the woman shuffled backwards, raising her arm to shut the door. "Try a little wine mixed with water and pray to Chemosh. I understand the king will offer a sacrifice tomorrow for those who are ill within the city. The gods should be pleased with such a public display of devotion."

Chemosh, the destroyer, the subduer of men, demanded only death, and already the city had lost enough people to the illness. Ruth jerked upright at the news. A sharp rebuttal burst from her lips. "No!"

For years, her parents had forced her to endure the ceremonies. She had been divided on whether to plug her ears with her fingers to shut out the wailing flutes and thumping drums or to cover her eyes from what would come next.

Mahlon did not worship Chemosh. With good humor, he tolerated his *imma's* evening stories about Yahweh's faithfulness. He was quick to agree with Naomi's teachings, but he never had the time or the interest to discuss anything deeper. However, Ruth drank in every single word of Naomi's, with a heart hungry for the Creator who offered deliverance. Stories of Abraham and the ram caught in the thicket. Moses escaping Egypt with the Israelites, guided at night by a pillar of fire. They calmed her troubled soul and brought a hope she had never known.

Yahweh wouldn't abandon her family now, would He?

At Ruth's outburst, the old woman slammed the door, leaving her alone in the alley with Orpah.

"It is too late," the young woman sobbed, wringing her hands in distress. "What can we do?"

"Pray to Yahweh for mercy," Ruth murmured as she clasped her sister-in-law's chilled hand and tugged her away from the barred door.

Surely, He would deliver mightily, just as He had in Naomi's stories. Surely, He would hear their cry.

As Ruth pushed open the door to her home, a guttural sound greeted her. She rushed into the cramped space, skidding to a halt when she spied Naomi crouched beside one pallet, pressing her fist against her mouth.

"Imma—" Orpah cried as she held back, holding a sleeve against her nose. The stench of sickness and sweat clung to the humid air, revolting after the breeze rustling through the street.

Staring at her husband, Ruth dropped to her knees beside Naomi.

No, not Mahlon.

Grief rose within her like a mighty wave, strong enough to send her rolling into its murky depths. With trembling fingers, she reached out to touch him, his beloved face finally at peace. Indeed, it seemed as if he only slept and both of them would soon awaken from this nightmare. Surely, she must be dreaming. Yet, in the corner of the room, a faint cough rattled from Chilion's chest, indicating that the nightmare was real enough.

"Mahlon died shortly after you left," Naomi whispered. She pulled the coarse blanket over him as if he were a child about to be tucked in before bedtime.

Ruth's throat and jaw tightened painfully. Why hadn't Yahweh at least allowed her to say goodbye to her husband?

When she spoke, she scarcely recognized her own voice. "I'm so sorry, Imma. The physician had left long before we reached his house. We rushed home as fast as we could."

If only we had left sooner.

But the fever had moved so quickly and attacked so many. And as Israelites in a Moabite city, Mahlon and Chilion were forced to wait for a healer.

Naomi snatched Ruth's hand, squeezing her fingers tightly, her expression bleak.

"We must tend to Chilion and do what we can." Naomi's voice was resigned, as if she feared the worst.

Ruth swept her husband's hair away from his forehead, now cool to the touch. She drew a deep, shuddering breath as she studied his features. Was it only a fortnight ago she had trimmed these shaggy locks, giggling while he snatched her hand to press a heated kiss against her palm? How could a fever snuff out a vibrant life so quickly? How could she live without him?

He never once made her feel inferior for being barren, even if she secretly grieved for a babe. Neither she nor Orpah had borne children. Now, her loss felt doubly painful. She had no bundle to hold close, no small, dimpled face to remind her of him.

Dazed, she tore herself from her husband's side to help Naomi bathe Chilion's forehead while Orpah shrank against the wall, weeping quietly. Ruth's hands shook as she poured tepid water onto a frayed linen cloth to wash Chilion's limbs. Her mother-in-law had long ago taught her to use water from a pitcher, clean and flowing, instead of letting it swelter in a basin for days. Naomi believed the practice brought health, as proclaimed by the priests of Yahweh. Tonight, the practice proved a futile exercise.

A flickering oil lamp cast a gruesome glow over the claustrophobic room. Chilion felt like fire, burning hotter and hotter despite the water droplets running down his flushed skin. His chest barely fluttered with life, each puff of air from his nostrils less and less.

An image of the bronzed Chemosh, with his rigid arms outstretched for sacrifice, flashed in Ruth's mind, while a great fire in the god's gutted belly roared and crackled, consuming everything given to it.

Please save Chilion for Naomi's sake. We cannot bear to lose anyone else this evening. It's too much loss for anyone to take.

Unlike Ruth's silent, frantic prayers as she wrung out the rag and washed him again, Naomi beseeched out loud, begging for the life of her remaining child. But as rosy dawn flooded through the open door, the battle was lost. Ruth bowed her head while Naomi keened with grief a second time, flinging herself across Chilion's chest. When Ruth tried to pull her mother-in-law away, Naomi resisted, clinging to her son's lifeless body.

Why hadn't the all-powerful Yahweh answered their prayers?

A Note from
THE EDITORS

We hope you enjoyed another exciting volume in the Extraordinary Women of the Bible series, published by Guideposts. For over seventy-five years, Guideposts, a nonprofit organization, has been driven by a vision of a world filled with hope. We aspire to be the voice of a trusted friend, a friend who makes you feel more hopeful and connected.

By making a purchase from Guideposts, you join our community in touching millions of lives, inspiring them to believe that all things are possible through faith, hope, and prayer. Your continued support allows us to provide uplifting resources to those in need. Whether through our communities, websites, apps, or publications, we inspire our audiences, bring them together, and comfort, uplift, entertain, and guide them. Visit us at guideposts.org to learn more.

We would love to hear from you. Write us at Guideposts, P.O. Box 5815, Harlan, Iowa 51593 or call us at (800) 932-2145. Did you love *Sins as Scarlet: Rahab's Story*? Leave a review for this product on guideposts.org/shop. Your feedback helps others in our community find relevant products.

Find inspiration, find faith, find Guideposts.

Shop our best sellers and favorites at

guideposts.org/shop

Or scan the QR code to go directly
to our Shop

Find more inspiring stories in these best-loved Guideposts fiction series!

Mysteries of Lancaster County

Follow the Classen sisters as they unravel clues and uncover hidden secrets in Mysteries of Lancaster County. As you get to know these women and their friends, you'll see how God brings each of them together for a fresh start in life.

Secrets of Wayfarers Inn

Retired schoolteachers find themselves owners of an old warehouse-turned-inn that is filled with hidden passages, buried secrets, and stunning surprises that will set them on a course to puzzling mysteries from the Underground Railroad.

Tearoom Mysteries Series

Mix one stately Victorian home, a charming lakeside town in Maine, and two adventurous cousins with a passion for tea and hospitality. Add a large scoop of intriguing mystery, and sprinkle generously with faith, family, and friends, and you have the recipe for *Tearoom Mysteries*.

Ordinary Women of the Bible

Richly imagined stories—based on facts from the Bible—have all the plot twists and suspense of a great mystery, while bringing you fascinating insights on what it was like to be a woman living in the ancient world.

To learn more about these books,
visit Guideposts.org/Shop